PAM K. [...]

THE GOLDEN LAND

THE GOLDEN LAND

By Edith Brockway

Illustrated by the Author

HERALD HOUSE, 1968

Contents

Chapter 1

The Storm

THE sky darkened over the marshes. The hot glitter of the afternoon was suddenly blotted out by a low mass of clouds moving southward. Shadows deepened among the reedbeds bordering the river; yellows turned to deep gold, and the brilliance of the whole valley, the marshes, the fields, and the city beyond dulled to somber hues beneath the spreading mass of clouds.

The boy crouching among the rushes did not notice the sky. Ori's brown face was turned downward, his eyes peering into the dark waters of the lagoon. His hand tightly clutched a three-pronged spear, ready to strike at any shadowy form which might dart into the open. He was not aware of the clouds, or of the wind swishing in the reedtops, or of his friend, Kib, resting on his spear, yawning.

"I'm tired of fishing here." Kib finally broke the silence. "This is not such a good place after all. We should go back where the goats are feeding." He was younger than Ori and less willing to stay in one position.

"You wait—one will come." Ori did not move. Despite the cramp in his legs he was determined to spear another fish before he left the place. "My brother Mahah has pulled some great ones from this lagoon. His boasting words will burn my ears if I don't do as well."

"Brothers are a nuisance," Kib answered. "I'm glad I have only sisters. If they scold me too much I pull their hair."

"And get slapped!" Ori straightened his slender body, then moved forward into the water. "But I would rather be slapped by my sister than by Mahah's words."

"Look there, beyond you!" Kib cried suddenly, pointing to an open break ahead of Ori. "Don't let him get away!"

A dark shadow slipped into the light. The silvery fish paused momentarily, just long enough for Ori to see it, then disappeared into the tangle of stalks. The boy waded knee-deep into the marsh, his spear high above his head, his heart beating excitedly.

But the gray form slipped away through the reeds, appearing, disappearing, darting in and out of the shadows. Ori dared not throw his spear until he could see the fish distinctly, fearing he would lose it entirely. He pushed on, farther and farther into the marsh, unmindful of the broken reed stalks cutting his feet, or the ankle-deep mud he was wading through, or the warnings of his mother to beware of wild boars feeding in the reeds.

Suddenly the fish darted into a shallow clearing and stopped. In an instant, Ori's spear shot forward, piercing the water with barely a ripple.

Swinging the impaled fish high above his head, Ori looked up at the sky. Now he saw the menacing clouds rolling high with the wind, and flocks of water birds, swept up from the marshes, flying southward. A flash of lightning snapped along the northern horizon, and thunder rumbled behind it. Gusts of cool air troubled the reedtops, and in their movement Ori felt a tingle of fear urging him to run.

"Kib!" he shouted into the wind. "Kib—where are you?" His words blew back into his face.

He remembered the goats. He and Kib had left the small herd feeding on young reed shoots along the eastern edge of the marsh before they started fishing. By now they could have wandered off out of sight.

Quickly Ori pushed the fish into the leather pouch strapped to his waist and, grasping his spear, plunged back through the reeds. Occasionally he stopped to look at the sky, then he would call—but only the swish of the reed tops and the crying of the birds answered him.

When he finally broke into the open, all that Ori could find was one fish still laying on the bank where they had left it. Kib and the goats were nowhere in sight. Ori scrambled out of the water, snatched up the fish, put it with the one in his pouch, and hurried to higher ground. He remembered a shallow cove where Kib liked to fish. Here in the springtime the water looked like a floating meadow, carpeted with white water buttercups. As he skirted the reeds at the end of the cove he saw the goats, then Kib coming excitedly toward him.

"I speared another fish!" He held up a shimmering prize. "You should come here—there are so many—but hard to hit unless you're fast." He looked at the bulge in Ori's pouch. "Did you get one big as mine?"

"Don't give mind to that!" Ori was out of breath . . . and patience. "Have you looked at the sky? The goats will be hard to drive in the rain."

Kib glanced up quickly, then back to his fish. "I am not afraid of a little rain. When it is over we can fish again."

"A little rain!" Ori jawed. "You have no eyes, and your ears are stopped with beeswax. Come on—help me with the goats."

Ori picked up a long reed and began swishing it at the brown and white spotted animals. They looked up from their feeding, their round eyes staring. They refused to move.

"Get behind them. Hit them with something!" Ori urged his friend.

But Kib, his mind on the fish he had seen in the cove, stood his ground. "I don't want to go home now. It's early yet."

"Stay and be drowned," Ori shouted angrily as he got behind the lead goat, Geme, and gave her a determined shove. He looked at the sky again and saw nothing but blackness. "You have forgotten how the river floods in the spring. If you stay here, the water will soon be lapping at your feet. Then the wild boar can come eat you for his supper."

The sound of thunder accentuated his words, and Kib, taking a longer look at the threatening sky and feeling a spat of water on his cheek, shouldered his spear. He flung his fish across the other shoulder and headed for the goats. He could feel the rain now.

The boys drove their herd east from the marshes through a rough growth of willows, past a scrub palm grove, then up over the shoulder of an embankment. Here, hollowed by the pressure of thousands of hooved and sandled feet, the road stretched northward into the city of Babil like the gouged trail of a giant serpent.

Other herds were on the road. Shepherds coaxed their baaing, restless flocks against the sting of the wind-driven rain with loud *huu-yahs* and the crack of long leather lashes. Dogs barked, and cries of confusion and distress fused in the wind. Sheets of rain obliterated the outline of the road, making it difficult for the shepherds to keep their course.

Ori and Kib tagged along behind, hurrying to keep in sight of the rest.

Suddenly the hard, fast beat of running hooves and the heavy rumble of rolling wooden wheels sounded behind Ori. He turned and saw a dark mass bearing down upon him.

"Kib!" he shouted wildly. "Move the goats out of the way!" He clawed through the rain, trying to get to the animals. They were right in the path of the oncoming sound. He looked back again.

A team of wild, dun-colored donkeys, called onagers, was headed toward him, pulling a heavy wooden chariot. Three men stood behind the brace—one driving, the others peering anxiously through the downpour.

One man in particular caught Ori's attention. He stood close behind the driver, his head and shoulders towering above

10

the others. His golden helmet glistened in the rain. When he saw the obstruction ahead of him, his voice bellowed out like the roar of a speared lion, demanding the shepherds and sheep to get out of his way. When this did not happen immediately, he uncoiled his whip from his girdle and released its length, cracking the air above Ori's head.

Ori leaped backwards, stumbling into Kib and the nearest goat, then fell sprawling into the wet slime of the road. Before he could right himself, he heard the whine of the whip again. He cried out, but the cutting leather hit his ewe, Geme, lifting a tuft of hair from her shaggy rump. She bolted forward, uttering a wailing blat as she climbed over the bodies of the slower moving sheep ahead of her.

Ori went sick with pain and anger. He started to spit out some bitter insult like he had heard his brothers use. But as the chariot came abreast of where he crouched he held his words, for the heavy black beard and golden helmet belonged to the overlord of the city.

It was Nimrod. This giant was stronger than ten men put together. He was fierce and cruel, a terror to neighboring cities and wandering tribes, for he brought all under his control. With the slaves he had captured, he had built Babil, the city of golden sunlight, between the rivers that flowed into the Sea of the Rising Sun. Here lay irrigated fields of wheat and barley, houses and walls built of sun-dried brick, a temple, and a great ziggurat. It was Etemenanki, the tower to link men of the earth with the gods of heaven. Nimrod was The Builder, The Great Hunter, The Protector of his people.

But to Ori, slowly bringing himself up out of the mud, he was a beast, a man who whipped boys and goats out of his way.

"If I was strong enough to carry a donkey load of grain on my shoulders, I'd not be afraid of that man," Kib whispered hoarsely as he and Ori stood watching the chariot move on through the herds.

"His heart is as black as his beard," Ori spoke bitterly. "How can my father stomach being a scribe to him? Day after day he has to write with a stylus what that lion roars out. I would die first." He bent to pick up his spear from the mud.

"A king has to be fierce." Kib turned his face to the rain. "I have decided that. Otherwise he could not bring in slaves to build great cities, or make the people obey him. I would rather be a king than a baker of barley cakes—like my father."

"You are baaing like a witless goat." Ori walked disdainfully ahead. "You could never be a king. Kings are cruel in battle, clever in their dealings with people. You might grow to be clever, but you are too softhearted to be fierce and cruel." There was a small pause. "It is better to be respected by the people . . . like my father. Although he is a servant to Nimrod, he is honorable and wise." His words whipped in the wind. "I want to be a scribe—but not to a man like Nimrod."

"Bakers and scribes—they are still servants." Kib persisted. "I want to be a king. And I will be. I will. I will." The words kept time with the pace of his feet and the intent of his dream.

The wind had died and the rain lessened to a drizzle when the boys heard the lashing of the date palm leaves in the groves outside the city. They crossed the footbridge of the southern canal, then prodded their goats into the street Enlil. They felt the comforting nearness of the wet-walled houses that hedged the narrow street. Passing tiny courtyards, fringed with pomegranate and plum, they splashed through the nauseant sweetness of decayed debris dumped underfoot, crisscrossed gardens of onion and fennel, bypassed the clay-brick silos where grain was flailed and stored, then came into the main street of the city.

All along the Great Way tradesmen had set their shops. Here strangers came at festival time to watch the processions of dancing girls and chanting priests. To the left, a brick wall edged the street, enclosing the gardens and courtyards of the temple and the half-finished ziggurat, Etemenanki.

12

Now the yawning stalls of the shopkeepers were empty. Instead of the usual crowd filling the street, only a few beggars huddled in the shelter of water-laden awnings. Temple pigeons cooed restlessly from a sheltered archway, and a dog howled mournfully in the distance. Kib moved closer to Ori as they neared the first temple gate.

"The wind-god Enlil is angry with us. That's why he sent this great storm." He looked furtively through the arched entrance to the temple where the god's shrine glistened in the rain.

"My father says that the rains come every year despite what the gods say." Ori spoke positively.

"You believe in the gods—don't you? Enlil and Enki and Ninhursaga—and all the demons?"

"My family prays to one God, Anu, Lord of all the universe."

The boys moved on beyond the gateway. Kib's face was troubled.

"Is your god Anu as great as Enlil, god of Babil?"

"Greater. My people have worshiped him for years, my grandfather and his—"

"You shouldn't say that!" Kib's voice was edged with anxiety. "If the temple priests hear that you worship this strange god they will bring some demon upon you. These demons will kill your goats or throw you in the river."

Ori looked sharply at his friend and said nothing. He knew that his father and mother were afraid of some of the priests for he had overheard their conversations—the great priest Nadu in particular. Nadu was greedy for influence in the temple, especially with the king, and Jared the scribe often stood in his way. Jared was a favorite of Nimrod.

The boys moved on to the second gateway in the wall. Looking through the great archway toward the mountainous ziggurat, Ori was surprised to see that hundreds of men were still working at the brick kilns. Great woven canopies had been stretched over the ovens where the facing bricks were being fired. Freemen and slaves were carrying the finished bricks up the slippery steps of the central stairway, up the second and third flights to the fourth wall. Here, in the heavy rain, other men were fitting the bricks into place and sealing them with reed matting and hot black pitch.

"They shouldn't be working now." Ori shivered as he watched. "The bricks will be ruined. They have tomorrow."

Kib pointed toward the men. "See there—it's Nimrod—forcing them to stay. Don't you see? They are trying to please Enlil. Enlil is angry because the tower is not finished for the festival of the New Year."

"Then Enlil is a tyrant too," Ori burst out as he watched Nimrod urge the men on with the crop of his whip. He thought he saw his father's brown tunic, but he wasn't sure. "I'm glad I don't worship Enlil."

"You'll be sorry for what you say," Kib scolded. "I will run home to make special prayers for you. With the proper offerings perhaps Enlil can forgive you—maybe even stop the rain."

Kib took one last look at the ziggurat and broke into a run, leaving his friend, his goats, and his fish behind.

Ori trudged on home, secured the goats in the reed-thatched shed, then opened the door into the courtyard, flung himself on a woolen mat close to a large water jar, and closed his eyes. He was exhausted.

Chapter 2

The Prophecy

THE sound of men's voices coming from the great room where the family met to eat and talk brought Ori's eyelids open again. It was the high flute-like voice of an old man that caught his attention. It was not rough and brusque like the voice of his grandfather Cham who lived far to the north. Nor did it have the gentleness of the older men who came to the house to visit with his father. It was shrill and intense.

"In the seventh moon all the windstorms of heaven attacked as one," the old one was saying. "The sky was awesome to behold when the south storm turned into blackness all that had been light; no one could see his fellow. Gathering speed, the flood winds blew until the rivers overflowed. The mountains submerged, and the land was as a sea."

His voice rose to a higher pitch as he spoke. Ori could barely understand all the words.

"When the sea grew quiet and the tempest was still and the floods ceased, I opened a hatch, and light fell on my face. I looked, then sat down to weep, for I saw that all mankind had turned to clay."

There was a long gasping sigh as though the speaker lacked the strength to continue. "The memories of those days are as bitter fruit for a man to remember."

"You have remembered them for a long time," came a stronger, heavier voice. It was Gilgah, younger brother of Jared, who often stopped to visit when his large reed rafts, or

15

keleks, were tethered along the river wharves. "I can remember when the spring floods flattened the grain fields and swept our crops into the sea. Not too many years ago my keleks were lost. They were carrying grain and oil down the Euphrates to the merchants of Eridu."

"This storm frightens you?" the old man asked.

"It is not good." Gilgah cleared his throat. "If it keeps raining I fear the city will become a lake with the people standing like bewildered sheep in the middle of it."

"Etemenanki will save us—Nimrod is seeing to that." A new voice spoke. It belonged to Ethem, dealer in grains. Ori knew him well, for he came often with Gilgah to talk with the men. "When his tower rises above the clouds, we will live with the gods in eternal sunlight." He laughed sharply.

"Small wonder we are not out there now working with the slaves."

"You will be too if your temple debts are not paid. Jared keeps an accounting of that."

Ori did not see the knowing wink which Gilgah passed to his friend as he rose to his feet, but he did sense that his uncle was jesting by the tone of his voice. "Let the tower be built to the glory of the gods. It may save us from drowning."

"You do not remember the ancient promise?" queried the old one.

Gilgah came to the doorway opening to the courtyard and paused. "If I once knew, I have forgotten."

"There will never be another flood as I knew it. The Creator made a vow through the sign of the rainbow that never again would he destroy mankind with water. Fire, yes, but never with water."

"Yes—yes, I remember now," Gilgah said. "My father told me years ago."

"But does Nimrod know that?" Ethem asked.

"I doubt it." Gilgah spread his hands. "Nimrod worships only the god of his own strength and wit. He knows the traditions of his ancestors which told of the flood, and he is angered by them. So he panders the superstitious beliefs of the people of Babil and makes a big show of building a tower to satisfy their gods, when in his heart he is defying them. You will see that, flood or no flood, Nimrod will prove he is stronger than all the gods put together, including Anu."

"Are you sure of this?" Ori's brother Jacom asked.

"Our family has known Nimrod since we drifted with the tribes along the steppes. Long ago I discovered that when he hunted or when he stopped to dream there was nothing in his mind but a desire to rule, to be stronger than anyone else. And he used many tricks to accomplish this. I learned to see through them, sometimes to my grief."

Ori sat up, for the words of his uncle meant something, particularly after what had happened on the road in the rain.

17

He had been right in his dislike of the king. Gilgah felt the same as he did, and that was important, for Gilgah was one he admired and respected, one he felt close to.

As he peered around the water jar toward the door of the great room, his uncle came across the court, stopped at the jar, and plunged the long-handled dipper down into the water. When Gilgah touched the rim of the cup to his lips he saw Ori.

"You are all right?" The man knelt by Ori's side, his eyes going over the drenched clothing and the wet, tousled hair.

"Kib and I brought the goats home. They are in the shelter." Ori saw the concern written in the man's lean face and was warmed by it.

"And you are like a drowned eagle." Gilgah pulled off the soggy linen tunic and replaced it with a coarse, brown woolen cloak. "Your mother has driven herself into the storm to look for you. She thinks you are still a boy, unable to take care of yourself. But here you are." Gilgah peered into the sodden leather pouch that Ori had dropped.

"Aiee—fresh fish for our empty bellies. And such big ones too. For such a beautiful gift you should be rewarded."

Ori's eyes widened. "Did you bring me a silver ring from Kish?"

"No rings from Kish." Gilgah put his thumb and forefinger together. "Only a pearl of my wisdom which you can wear with pride—or throw to the winds."

"I will wear it," Ori agreed hastily, anxious to hear more.

"It will make your head grow like a melon," Gilgah grinned, then his face sobered. "You are much like your father, given to serious thoughts despite your twelve years. You are quick to learn. I have seen your work with the stylus, and it is good. You are a friend to many. You are impulsive at times, strong tempered, but in the right place. This is worthy." The big man's hand gripped Ori's arm. "Someday, if you set your mind to it, you will be a leader of men, respected, looked up to. This will not be easy, but its value is more than that of a silver ring. You agree?"

Ori nodded, not fully aware of all the implications of his uncle's words. "Kib wants to be a king. Should I want to be a king rather than a scribe?"

"The kings I know are greedy and vain. These are not qualities of greatness." Gilgah stood erect, his eyes smiling. "Come in with the others. I will show you a man who has been favored with many gifts, more than any king."

The only light in the great room came from the center of the mat-covered floor. Here a yellow-white flame tipped with smoke flared from the pinched spout of a shallow, oil-filled dish. The glow softly outlined the painted panels on the walls, the shelves stacked with fine pottery. It lit up the loom where Ori's sisters sat listening to the man-talk, and the circle of men's faces as they sat about the room.

Jacom, Ori's oldest brother, sat near the doorway on a large cushion. He worked with Gilgah at the grain market, and his stylus and clay tablets were spread around him on the floor. Across from him, lying on his stomach, was Ori's other brother, Mahah, teasing a cockroach with a bit of reed. He was only two years older than Ori, was taller and of a heavier build, but since he had begun his apprenticeship with the temple silversmith he considered himself above any companionship with his younger brother.

Beyond Jacom sat Ethem, his head wound in a woolen scarf, and to his left was the Ancient One.

Ori bowed to them all, but the old man perched on a stool like a wizened bird—half in shadow, half in light—fascinated him, for he had never seen such a person before. Bright, penetrating eyes peered out at him from deep sockets above a thin, flaring nose. The old man's skin was withered as old leather etched with tiny wrinkles. His mouth cut a sharp line between his shallow cheeks, and long white hair hung in wisps about his neck and chin.

Gilgah touched the ancient's bone-thin hand.

"This is Jared's youngest son, Orihah. He is a shepherd

19

boy, but someday when he has learned all the characters he can be a scribe—possibly to a king." He winked at Ori.

"He has chosen well." A light flickered momentarily in the old man's eyes as he gazed at the boy. "We have been taught from the beginning to read and write. It is part of our great heritage." He reached out and grasped Ori's hand. "But this boy will do more than write for kings. I see that he will find his place beyond the realms of the river lords."

"Is there such a place?" Jacom asked in surprise.

"Our world has many faces, my son. Many you will never see." The Ancient One closed his eyes and seemed barely to breathe. Then his voice came again—faint, yet with conviction. "After the floods slipped back into the seas, the Creator showed me many lands that he had made. They are covered with forests and flowers and rivers running as silver through the mountains. There are wide valleys and great plains dotted with blue seas."

The room was very still. The listeners waited, eager to hear more, but the old man seemed lost in a dream. His eyes closed.

"Does he mean that I might see one of these lands?" Ori whispered to Gilgah after a long pause.

"Patience. He will speak again. And listen carefully, for his wisdom is great."

Finally the weathered head lifted, and the eyes opened wide. "Now the ancient image is fresh in my mind just as it has appeared so often during the many years. There is one land that stands alone amid the great waters, golden in the sunlight. This is a choice place for choice people. Would that I could see it before I die." He shook his head sadly. "I fear I never will."

"Where is this place? Could we take you there?" Gilgah asked.

A sharp laugh issued from the old man's throat. "And how would you get me to it—with a thousand seraph's wings?"

Then he sobered, his sharp eyes going from one to the other of the people in the room. "I am the stupid one. You offer to take me there, and according to the vision your faces are the ones I saw."

"What are you saying?" Gilgah crouched by the withered body.

"I saw a tribe of people being led by a divine power out across a great expanse of space to find this land, across the land and across the seas, through time and hardships. You are that people, Gilgah, you and Jared. I recognized it first here in the boy. I have seen his face in the vision."

The sound of his voice rang in the room. Ori felt a tingling sensation around the roots of his hair and down his arms. He stared at the old man as at an oracle from heaven—believing, yet unbelieving. The whole idea was so unreal, so foreign to anything that had happened thus far in his life. It must be true for it followed what Gilgah had said—about his being a leader—and Gilgah was not one to talk lightly of important things. Ori respected the words of his uncle and his own inner feelings of what was right.

"Does this mean we will leave Babil?" he asked Gilgah timidly.

The crouched figure raised, went to the doorway, then turned, facing the room. Gilgah's eyes were dark and luminous.

"If we are commanded to leave, we will leave."

"Think of it not as a command but as an opportunity," the old man whispered audibly. "You will become a great nation, spreading from sea to sea."

A rustling noise at the front entrance of the house pulled Ori's thoughts away from the words that had been spoken. He became conscious again of the rain, for he heard its sound coming through the outside door. He looked around to see his mother standing by Gilgah's side, pulling her dripping cape from her head. When Mari saw his face in the lamplight her body relaxed and the look of anxiety disappeared from her eyes.

"I was afraid you were lost in the storm." She came to touch his damp curls and rest her hand on his shoulder as she looked around the room. "Thank heavens we are all here—all but your father. I could hear the rushing river. It frightens me. We may have to spend the night out on the plain."

"We could go to the roof," Ori assured her. "Our house is strong."

"And be left like geese in a tree?" She turned to Gilgah. "And what of your children and Timna?"

"Time is a bird that flies away much too quickly." He looked for his woolen shawl. "My brood was safe when I left it . . . but my keleks . . . they must be tied higher on the shore." He looked to Ethem. "Coming with me?" Then he turned back where the old man sat with his head bowed over his chest.

"Are you asleep, ancient father? I must tend my keleks or they will be swept away. I shall remember what you said."

The white head nodded, the long fingers reached out in a gesture of dismissal. "Ask the Great Father for direction. He will tell you where to go." His head dropped again, and his eyes closed.

Mari, sensitive to some strange atmosphere in the room, asked Gilgah, "What is he talking about—where do you need to go?"

"Ori will tell you, ask him." Gilgah shouldered his shawl. "Just remember that no matter what happens, everything that has been said will come to pass. I know it."

"We are to leave Babil and go to a new land," Ori burst out.

"And what of Jared?" Mari's eyes went wide. "How can he leave his work?"

"What has he to lose?" Ethem broke into the conversation as he headed for the door. "He is nothing but a slave to Nimrod—working for that madman during this storm. And it is no secret that the great priest resents your husband's pres-

22

ence in the temple. The idea of going grows brighter in my mind. I like it."

Mari went pale about her mouth and turned her back to the group. "You all must have lost your senses. You should not speak so before the children."

"It is a divine will that tells us this," Ori assured his mother. "The Ancient One has seen it."

"It is more than I can understand," Mari exclaimed, facing them again. "All this—and the rain, and Kib's mother making prayers to Enlil."

There was a sudden shouting in the street outside.

Ori jumped to his feet and hurried through the court to the front entrance.

People were running through the rain, calling to each other. A chariot came in sight and the cries of "The river is flooding—the river is coming upon us. Run . . . run . . . the river is coming . . . the river . . ." echoed through the street.

Doors burst open and women and children ran out of their houses, looking toward the north and west, for their homes lay only a short distance from the wharves.

"My rafts . . . my keleks . . ." Gilgah shouted as he ran past Ori, with Ethem fast behind him. "My keleks will be washed into the sea."

"And what of this family?" Mari was behind Ori, and her fingers dug into his shoulders. "What shall we do without a father?"

They could hear the flood's voice now, the long sustained roar of water as it rushed past the date groves to the north, the wharves and markets to the west. The canals, built to deflect waters from the city, were full and overflowing. Soon the muddy, whorling deluge would be creeping into the streets and lapping at the doorsteps.

Feeling his mother's desperation through her fingers, Ori burned with the hot coal of what he should do. He pulled himself away from her grasp and ran into the street toward Etemenanki.

23

Chapter 3

The Flood

THE wind had died down, but the rain still came in a steady downpour as Ori dodged down the narrow streets, splashing through puddles of water and debris and by-passing small huddled groups of frightened people. Out of breath, he finally came to the northern gate of the tower wall and turned toward the kilns where the brickmakers were working.

As he drew nearer, Ori saw that the scene had changed. Now the kilns were surrounded with women and children. They stood in groups facing the men, calling to them, urging them to leave their work, despite the angry words of the temple guards. The men were going through the motions of working, their faces sullen and fearful, their minds desperate to be free.

Ori edged through the crowd looking for the familiar brown tunic of his father, Careful not to attract the attention of the temple guard, he darted to the back of the kilns under the shelter of the great canopy. Here the bricks were being loaded on long tent-like racks to be carried to the top of the tower. Two men bent over a pile of surfacing bricks, moving them one by one onto the rack. They were evidently slaves, for the brand of the temple was upon their shoulders.

Timidly Ori came close to one and touched his arm lightly. "Have you seen Jared, the scribe?"

The man looked sharply at the boy, then pointed to the top of the four levels of the ziggurat. "Up there. He is counting the measurements of pitch."

Ori looked up through the rain. Only a dim outline of the great mountain of earth could be seen, and its awesome nearness sent a tremor of excitement through his shoulders and down to his fingertips. He had never been so near Etemenanki before. His father had forbidden his coming within the temple walls, for the temple, the tower, and the surrounding courts were used primarily by the king and the priests. The people of the city were allowed to enter only during the times of religious rituals and festivals; otherwise their presence might offend the gods.

Despite his fear of being seen, Ori slipped from beneath the canopy and ran toward the great stairway, a wide procession of steps that stretched up the center and to the top of the first level of the tower. His legs weakened as the steps grew steeper, and by the time he had reached the upper terrace he had to stop and rest. Workmen, returning from the second level, looked suspiciously at him but moved on without speaking. He followed a couple of brick carriers up one of the two narrower stairways that hugged the wall of the second level.

It was when he had crossed the width of the second terrace that Ori stopped to lean his back against the wet glazed tile of the massive wall of the next level. Looking toward the west he saw the river spreading over the land in a wide yellow swath of rushing muddy water. Ori had never been so high before. Now he could see the land and the flood in one awesome glance.

Two figures came hurrying down the steps from the upper level. One of them stopped when he saw the boy gazing intently at the river.

"Orihah, what are you doing here?"

Ori looked up, startled, for he had momentarily forgotten why he was there. Seeing his father's face he hesitated to speak, fearing the older man's anger, for his full name Orihah was seldom spoken.

"The river . . ." he groped about for words. "The river is flooding, and we were frightened. We will all be swept away if you are not home to help us. The Ancient One is there . . . and the goats . . . they can't sleep on the roof." Little bursts of words tumbled out as Ori sought his father's sympathy.

"Is this your son, Jared?" The voice of the second person broke in. "He should be home with his mother."

Ori looked up, embarrassed that the speaker had not noticed that he was big enough to take care of himself. It was Nimrod, hooded with a cloak, his great body standing as a bastion against the rain, his figure as monumental as the tower itself. Ori flattened himself against the wall, wishing he could disappear into the brick facing. Too vividly he remembered the crack of the whip and the tufts of wool lifted from Geme's back.

Jared looked from the boy's frightened face to that of the overlord, then down to the flooding river. "My son is frightened by the thought that soon the river will spread over the city until the fields and houses will be as little islands without life. The women and children will be gone to the plains, and the men will be as wolves fighting for their whelps."

"They will receive their pay; you will see to that." Nimrod turned away from them, then stopped. "This is no time for men to be entangled with women's work. The wives are strong-backed. They can take the children and leave. If the flood covers the city this time, all the more reason that the tower be finished before we are all drowned in the next great deluge. The men must stay."

"How many bricks can be made when the river is among us? How much higher will the wall go tonight while women and children fight against mud and water with their bare hands? Men are not made of clods of beaten earth." Jared's voice grew flint-hard as he spoke.

The great man turned to the river, then back to his scribe. "Ever since we used to hunt together as boys, you and Gilgah

26

could tangle me in a snare of words if you so minded. You are still doing it, and I respect you for it, even though I have resented it all my life." Nimrod wrapped his robe about him more closely. "So . . . what is your plan? I know you have one or you wouldn't be standing there, blazing away like a fiery seraph."

The tense lines of Jared's face relaxed. He reached out and pulled his son to him, wiping the rain from the boy's face with a wet sleeve. "The tower can give shelter to the people

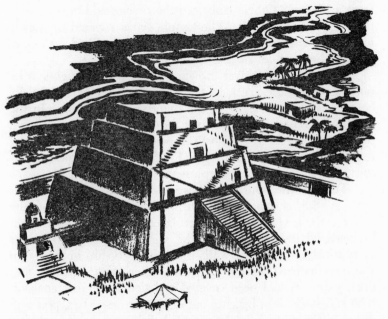

until the flood has receded. It is built high above the river, and if its doors are opened now the people will bless you. Men will work in the tomorrows' suns, and Etemenanki will stand yet as a monument to your wisdom."

Nimrod stared blankly at Jared for a few seconds, rubbed his dripping beard with a heavy thumb, then turned toward the stairway leading downward. "You have said it, Jared.

Now make it so. As for me, I must go pray to some agreeable god who will forgive my sins of weakness."

The grip on Ori's shoulder tightened, then relaxed, and the slender fingers of the scribe grasped those of his son as the two silently followed the wide back of the builder until he disappeared into a room of the level below. Then quickly they descended the steps and proceeded toward the kilns.

The words that passed from Jared to the overseers spread as wildfire among the sullen men. Many sped from the spot as from a plague. Others embraced their wives and hurried with them toward the street. The temple slaves covered the newly fired brick and closed the kiln doors, for they had no homes outside the confines of the wall.

The roar of the river drowned all of Ori's thoughts as he ran with his father back to their home. They paused briefly before the door to listen to the thunder of the flood. In the growing darkness they could see the water as it crept through the shallow levels to the north, spreading into the streets, surrounding houses, and lapping at the feet of a few curious persons who stood awed at its presence.

Tearing their attention away, the man and boy went through the entrance into the darkened courtyard of the house. By now the upper dirt layer of the roof had been loosened by the pounding of the rain, and rivulets of water came trickling down the walls through the breaks in the palm- and reed-thatched ceiling. All the woolen mats, cushions, and linen garments had been covered and tied in a great goatskin robe and stacked on benches out of the wetness. Jars, pots and dishes, sacks of grain and fruit, Ori's fish, and the red cooking brazier were caught in several reed nets and suspended from the rafters of the Great Room.

The women of the house, their eyes pained with uncertainty, their long dresses splotched with water, stood holding a heavy reed mat above the sleeping figure of the Ancient One. Jacom was gone. In the courtyard Mahah struggled with a long rope, endeavoring to tie the restless goats together.

Jared called to his family. "We may not have this much of a home awaiting us when another dawn breaks again, but tonight—if we move quickly—we will not have to sleep in the rain."

"I prayed you would know a way." Mari's voice sang with hope. "We were so afraid the boy would not find you. Jacom went too, but I am not always so sure of Jacom now that he has found a girl to love." A shaded concern crept into her eyes. "Where do we go, Jared?"

"The gods of Babil are sharing their beds with us," the scribe said wryly as he set about making a litter for the sleeping holy man. "They have decreed that their wings of compassion will be spread over the little people of the city and will shelter them in their 'holy of holies.' "

"Jared, you didn't . . ."

"No, I didn't! It was Nimrod who prayed their forgiveness."

"Fear sickens me when you speak lightly of the gods in the presence of the priests. It's a wonder that you have remained in the temple so long—being an unbeliever."

"Nimrod respects my words. The priests are afraid of Nimrod, and Nimrod is afraid only of himself." The scribe finished tying a large reed mat between the length of several fishing spears. "I watch my words . . . but it is only through the Lord's mercy that I am untouched."

He brought the litter in beside the Ancient One and waved Mahah to his side. Together they lifted the frail body onto the mat and covered it with a woolen cloth. As they raised the litter between them and started for the door, Jared called to the rest.

"Bring what you can carry on your backs—the pottery and woolens. And you, Ori, bring the goats. The rest will be left to whatever fate awaits it." He turned directly to his wife. "And, Little Mother, Jacom is old enough to find his way through the rain."

Ori was the last to leave. When the last shaggy goat had passed through the door, he shut it carefully behind him, silently praying that by some miracle his home would remain as he had left it.

It was when the family of Jared neared the gate north of Etemenanki that an enveloping fear of the flood overtook them.

Hundreds of desperate people from the narrow back streets, driving their animals ahead of them, were crowding the entrances into the tower area. The rain had abated to a mist-like drizzle, but this did not keep the sea of water from creeping toward the slope back of the tower walls and edging its way up the side streets. Lamenting cries from the women, echoed by the children, rose above the men's hoarse shouts and the bawls of frightened animals.

Ori pulled his goats closer to him, urging them into the massing stream of humanity that pushed toward the gate. Seeing the crowd, he feared that he and his family would be crushed in the passageway. He thought of the Ancient One and what great sorrow it would bring should the frail body of this holy man be trampled under the pounding feet of the mob. He wondered suddenly why it was that the old man had been with them on that particular day. Where had he come from?

Ori's mother looked anxiously behind her at her youngest son, readjusted the goatskin bundle on her shoulders, and called for him to hurry. They must stay together.

The heavy breathing of a large animal came up behind Ori, and he turned in time to sidestep the long curving horns of an oncoming cow. Behind her came her calf, edging her flank. In the pressure of the crowd, Ori felt himself and his goats pushed against the calf, just behind the swing of the menacing horns, and carried forward in a living avalanche through the passageway of the gate into the courtyard beyond. Here he could breathe again; the cow and calf passed on, but the members of his family had disappeared in the surging mass.

In a desperate effort to find refuge above the rising flood waters, the refugees swept toward the great stairway of the ziggurat. When they reached the rows of the lower steps, they looked upward and saw coming slowly toward them down the great incline a procession of temple priests, chanting their prayers to the gods, their shaven heads gleaming in a forest of lighted torches. Before them came the throne bearers, carrying the golden image of the god, Enlil. To the right of the god walked the great priest Nadu, carrying the sacred bucket for the sacrificial ritual. To the left danced the chief chanter, beseeching Enki, god of the waters of Abyss, to save Babil from the demons of disaster. Rows of chanters, diviners, and musicians followed close behind, repeating the cry.

The crowd, awed by the sight, pushed backward into the court, making a wide passageway for the procession as it slowly descended and stopped at the base of the stairway.

Ori tried to edge forward for a closer view of the ritual, but too many people were standing in front of him, chanting and waving their arms. Their bodies rocked back and forth as they called upon the gods.

"My god, I would stand before you.
I would speak to you—my word is a groan.
Evil fate holds me in its hand, carries off my breath of life.
My god, you who are my father, who begot me, lift my face.
How long will you neglect me, leave me unprotected."

Then followed a long roll on the drum, accented by the staccato beat of the timbrels. The great priest Nabu, holding high his holy bucket, summoned the builders of the sacrificial fires. The people stopped their chanting, lowered their arms, and with bowed heads slowly knelt in the slippery mud.

Ori hugged his goats close to him. He knew what was coming. They were to slay a sacrifice. A brown kid was brought from the temple sheds. A black-robed priest came forward with a gleaming knife to slash the kid's throat. Ori hid his face in the long hair of Geme's side and shut his eyes.

31

It was not until he heard the drums again and the crackling of the fire as it leapt upward through the tinder of the pyre that Ori lifted his eyes. Nabu was pouring the purification milk from his sacred bucket over the slain sacrifice. Then he raised his arms to heaven and shouted:

"O thou father of the gods, king of heaven and earth; our tears, our anguish beseech thee to accept this offering. Send again the rays of the sun-god Utu to comfort us."

The chanters took up the cry; the drums rolled; the harps and timbrels twanged. As wheat blown before the wind, the wailing worshipers flung themselves before their god.

Ori found himself standing conspicuously above the multitude. He looked furtively around, fearful that he was doing something wrong. Far to the right, near the northern wall of the court, Ori saw the members of his family, huddled together, erect and immobile. The Ancient One was standing on his feet now, leaning heavily on Jared's arm. Ori wanted to shout to them, but he feared his voice would ring out above the wails of the worshipers. If it were not for the goats he would step over rows of prone bodies that separated him from his family, but he dared not. Even if he waved, here in the semidarkness he might attract the attention of the chief chanter and the high priest Nabu. They were busy scanning the crowd for any sign of disrespect to the ritual. Ori crouched down among the goats, hoping he would not be seen. He wished that his father would kneel out of sight or hide behind a cow, but he knew the tall, straight-backed scribe would not bow down to the golden image of an earthly god.

At a shout from Nabu, a diviner—resplendent in an embroidered tunic—came forward to give the message from the god. Enlil was pleased with the sacrifice and would send no more rain. The people should rejoice and give offerings of grain and silver to the temple in thanksgiving for this favor.

The ritual completed, the crowd raised to its knees, then to its feet, and stood solemnly waiting for the procession of priests to move from the tower court into the adjoining temple.

32

Chapter 4

The Threat

ORI, pulling his goats closely behind him, pushed his way into the human tide moving toward the north wall. But the refugees meshed as they reached the great stairway and carried the boy and goats up the steep slippery steps.

Seeing an unoccupied alcove in the wall ahead of him, Ori urged his goats forward, hoping that here he might catch a glimpse of his family. His mind ached from the strain of searching. Forcing the goats against the wall, he slid down

among them and, lulled by the shuffling of passing feet, fell asleep. So deep was his sleep that he did not hear the rain begin again.

But another noise did awaken him. Half awake and half asleep, he became conscious of two men talking softly, so as not to be overheard. Opening his eyes, Ori saw that they wore the red woolen tunics of the temple guards. Low burning torches burned fitfully in their hands.

"They are here somewhere. The flood waters are seeping into the lower courtyards now. Most of the outside entrances are blocked, except the East Gate. What man, except he be driven by a thousand demons, would venture out into the flood?" spoke one of the men.

"Are the waters so high?" came the second voice.

"I felt with my feet and saw with the light of my torch that the tower is an island in an angry sea. The great priest sent me into all the recesses of the outer wall—even to the market stalls—looking for the unbelievers. It is because they have defied Enlil and brought the rains again that the veins on the neck of his lordship stood out and his face flamed red with anger." The speaker cleared his throat. "You have not found the scribe in the tower?"

"I searched the storerooms of grain and oil, the cattlesheds and stables, even the cellars. It is easier to pluck gold from the sand than to pick a man's face from the crowd that fills the tower rooms. We must wait for the morning."

"Don't you fear the anger of Nabu? He does not tolerate disappointment."

"We can make the excuse that the demons of night were released before the offenders were found."

"Hah! You do not know the mind of the high priest." The voices moved on around the wall. "You take the stairway to the left, I to the right. Demons or no demons we must bring . . ." the rest of the sentence was lost in the sound of the rain.

Ori sat staring into the night. He wanted to run some-

34

where and hide in the dark where he could cry and his mother would hear him and bring food and a dry mat to sleep on. If he cried here, then his father might come, and the temple guards would return and carry his father away to some strange place where the high priest would pour the sacred milk over him and burn him as a sacrifice.

With a little cry, Ori buried his face in his arms and shook with fright. If only he could find his father and warn him. Then he remembered that Gilgah and the Ancient One talked to Anu when they needed help. Perhaps Anu could hear him. Slowly little thoughts took shape, thoughts of praise for their deliverance from the storm, that the Ancient One had not been crushed in the mob. Then he asked that his father might be protected from the temple guards, that he . . .

"So, you prefer a cold wet wall to a warm woolen bed!" A voice joked at the praying boy. Firm fingers reached beneath Ori's chin and tilted his head toward the torchlight. It was his uncle Gilgah. "I think you prefer the rain to freshly broiled fish. If it had not been for Geme here, looking at me so sorrowfully with her great eyes and full udders, I would have passed by."

Encircling the boy's shoulders with one hand and propelling the goats with the other, Gilgah moved up the stairway to the next terrace. Fear made a hard knot inside Ori as they went upward, for he expected to see the torch of the temple guard coming toward them. Seeing none, he finally ventured a question.

"Where is the fish and the warm woolen mat? Are my mother and father with them?"

"They are all together, out of the rain," Gilgah answered.

"But where did you find them? I saw them by the north wall—then they were gone. I waited by the stairway, but they did not come."

"I have sharp eyes. I saw you both when all the worshipers kissed the earth. Who else would be standing erect at such a time except those of us who do not believe in the gods?"

35

There was a stretch of silence as they moved upward. "I also saw the angry face of Nadu when we did not grovel in the mud."

"I know," Ori broke in excitedly. "I heard the temple guard speaking of the priest's anger. They were looking for my father. I know he is the one they blamed for the rain coming again." Ori's voice sharpened. "What kind of punishment is there for those who do not worship the gods?"

"Time will bring that answer," Gilgah replied grimly.

Gilgah did not stop on the second level but turned to the third flight of stairs. The light from the torches below faded and disappeared as the two groped their way upward through the rain. Ori could hear the rushing river below and imagined that one misstep might send him downward into the swirling deluge. Out of breath, he stopped at the top of the stairs to look back at the courts below. The red tunic of a temple guard passed into the light, then out again.

The man and boy worked their way along the wall of the fourth level toward a small door. Pushing it open, they stepped into a small room illuminated by the fires of several braziers. Around one brazier sat the family of the scribe: his wife Mari, Mahah, two daughters, and the Ancient One. Beyond them, with their separate fire, grouped the family of Ethem: his wife, his three sons and two daughters. Among the others, Ori recognized the faces of those who came at times to worship with their family, Omer and his wife, a daughter about his own age, then younger boys and girls.

Gilgah's wife, Timna, arose when she saw her husband, and stepped from her family group when he spoke.

"I return one of your sons, but not the other," Gilgah sang out as he grasped Timna about the waist, then turned to Jared. "I heard through Ubara the tanner that a young man of the stand of Jacom was seen trailing the family of Lugalbanda— who has a lovely daughter."

Small laughter passed through the group. Mari, her eyes puddled with tears, came to clasp her youngest son to her in

36

a quick embrace. Placing a bowl of broiled fish in his hand, she led him to a cushion by the light. It was after she had milked Geme and the other she-goats and served everyone with bowls of foamy yellow milk that she dropped beside Ori, her hands upturned in her lap, her eyes questioning.

"I was so afraid the temple guards would find you that I cried." Ori's voice sounded small in the space around it. "Then I remembered to pray. God does listen, doesn't he?"

"Yes, son." Jared answered instead of his mother. "But why did you fear the guards? Was Nimrod wanting me?"

"Not Nimrod—the high priest Nabu," Gilgah broke in.

"I overheard two guards talking. I know they were looking for you, Father, for they sought those who would not kneel during the sacrifice." Ori's voice trembled. "But since you are hidden here, away from the torches, they will not find you, will they?"

"We came to this room not to hide but to find a night's rest," Jared answered quietly. "A man can barely stand, let alone sleep, on the levels below. I have been here many times to count the supplies of straw and pitch stored by the brick makers."

"Do you know the fate of those who defy the gods?" Gilgah stretched himself beside Timna on a pile of straw and cupped his hands behind his head. "Perhaps the most they would do is send a few demons into our houses to whistle at us."

"I have seen men, even chieftains, imprisoned in the lower rooms of the temple. They were sent there not only as captives from the wars of Nimrod but by command of the high priest."

"Oh, Jared!" Mari's face went white. "Where shall we go?"

There was silence, the question hanging unanswered in the air, for no one dared define a future that stood as a darkened room before them. The Ancient One, stretched on a mat next to Mahah, raised himself on a bony elbow and scratched the fringes of his beard. Clearing his throat, he said rebukingly, "Your minds are tired or you would remember where you are to go."

"Do you speak of Mount Sephar, far to the east, holy father?" Jared turned to the old man. "Should we go with you back to your homeland?"

"Oh, no, he doesn't mean that, Father." Ori broke in excitedly, for he suddenly remembered the words of the prophecy spoken by the Ancient One earlier that afternoon. " 'There is a land standing alone beyond many waters—that lies golden in the sunlight.' That is the place where we are to go."

Jared moved his eyes questioningly from the boy to the faces turned to him; they *had* momentarily forgotten those words of promise. "You all agree to what the boy says? He is not speaking a fable?"

"It is no fable, my son," the old man said. "Have you asked why I am here—why I came to your house before the storm?"

Jared's eyes widened, but no words came from his mouth. There had been no time for questions.

"I have seen this same vision many times in the past," the thin voice went on, "but today it came to me brilliant as a polished stone. In his vast wisdom, our great Lord calls his children away from the worship of man-made gods. He scatters them across the face of the earth as seeds before the wind, sowing a harvest of nations. I came to tell you this, for you are part of his children. You are to leave the wickedness of Babil."

Jared stared at the old man, his face a confusion of thought. "If what you say is true, where is this land . . . how do we go there . . . when do we leave—in a day, a month, a year? Do we go alone or with our friends? Will the Lord send us a sign to follow?" He shook his head stubbornly. "This burden you bring is heavy to bear."

The bony hands spread wide. "You have only to believe. You will be led—don't doubt that. And when? I only know I felt a prick in my mind to hurry here today to tell you this. As to your friends," the frail body leaned back on the straw and the eyes closed, "though I saw your faces clearly, I was aware that there were many more . . . many more believers in the Lord."

Gilgah's body jerked upward from the straw floor as his thoughts took shape. "This is a warning, Jared. If the temple guards are looking for us, we are in danger. Why else would the Ancient One have come?"

"You mean we should go out into the night, out into the storm?" Mari's voice rose with the climbing of her fear.

"Nabu has us in a trap . . . a very convenient one," Gilgah continued. "It could be that the flood has given him an excuse to rid himself of an unwanted scribe."

"Nimrod would not allow such a thing to happen." Jared's back straightened. "He has always stood between me and the priest's petty schemes."

"If he knows about them, you mean."

"Nimrod has many spy-servants. He would find out what Nabu is doing."

"You are the confident one. I am of Mari's mind. If it were not for the flood, I would leave this place tonight." Gilgah stood up and paced back and forth across the straw.

Jared paled, and the lines of his jaw hardened. "You have let this old man sway you with his words." He nodded toward the prone figure of the Ancient One, then lowered his voice. "How can his visions of a faraway land force us from our home? We belong here in Babil, you know that. You act like a superstitious follower of Enlil—afraid of the demons."

Ori stared at his father, then at his uncle, and his loyalties were torn between the two. He wanted to believe the logic of his father, to share the confidence he felt in his king, but when Ori thought of Nimrod's brutality, his overbearing bigness, he shrank with fear. Perhaps the old man's vision of the land was a superstition, just as Kib's believing in the power of Enlil to bring the storm. Yet Gilgah's point of view was not to be taken lightly. He had made mistakes, but not when it came to obeying the divine will, or knowing good answers to troubling questions. Finally a burning thought came to Ori's mind. "Father," he spoke timidly at first, then seeing that Jared did not pay attention, he repeated his word, louder. "Father, we must ask the Lord's help."

Jared swung around to look at his son, and the sternness went out of his face. His eyes gentled, and a troubled hand brushed back a strand of hair from his forehead.

"Yes, yes, that is what we must do." He looked again at Gilgah, as though he had never spoken out against the faith of his brother. "You must cry out to the divine will, asking for help, else we will walk in fear."

The heavy framed figure of the boatman turned to face the group, and Ori, looking up, saw his eyes catch the light from the brazier, saw his cropped hair turn red-bronze and his shoulders straighten as his head went up. There was a power here which the boy could not describe, an intangible force that changed doubt into confidence; where there had been fear, now there was hope and strength.

At the close of the prayer Ori felt his father's hand reach across him to touch his mother's shoulder. He felt the tensing of the muscles in the strong arm as the man shared his reassurance with his wife.

"Now I can face any man," Jared stated simply, "unafraid."

Chapter 5

The Trial

T HE mist-pearled glow of another day came through the small door of the upper room and awakened Ori. Confused at first as to where he was, he scrambled to his feet and stood for a moment, hesitant and dizzy. A small fire glowed in the red brazier, outlining the empty mats strewn about the room. The men were gone, except the Ancient One who still slept on a straw mat close to the back wall. Following the pale glow of daylight, Ori went out the door onto the damp terrace and crossed to the outer wall, where he looked down on the scene below.

Dark gray clouds, still heavy with rain, moved southward above him, adding a murky drabness to the roiled colors of the lake of water that spread itself across the length of the river valley. Buildings, which had crumbled away by the undermining action of the water, stood as aged cheeses in a giant dish of brown broth. The wharves where the trader's boats were usually tied, the keleks and coracles, the flimsy market stalls were no more. Debris from the backwash of the current was strewn into the water-filled streets, and among the floating timbers and matted trash were the bodies of drowned cattle and sheep.

Tearing his eyes away, Ori looked at the terraces below and saw hundreds of Babilians standing along the walls, hypnotized like himself by the spectacle below them. His eyes were drawn to a small figure on a lower level, standing alone and waving to him. It was Kib.

Quickly the boys spanned the time and space that divided them, and breathing heavily, they raced toward each other.

"You're here," Ori yelled out, glad to see his friend. "Did your house get washed away—or your cow?" He was remembering the dead animals in the water. Then he noticed Kib's expression of fear and anxiety. "What's happened?" Kib came close and looked reassuringly into the face above him. "Don't be afraid of me—I won't tell them where you are."

There was a small silence while Ori rearranged his thoughts, his brows furrowing. Slowly his words took shape. "Tell *who* where I am?"

"The temple guard, or any of the priests. When I came by the great stairway this morning I saw your father and your uncle and several other men marching down, surrounded with guards. They were on their way to the temple."

"That is not so unusual." Ori sought to cover his fears with casual words. "My father goes every day to the temple—with or without the temple guards."

"But this was different. The guards were carrying spears. I heard the people talking and they said that your father had cast a magic spell over the king, making him staring-blind."

"That is not true." Ori's face went white around the flare of his nose. "You know that is not true—it couldn't be. These people who talk are like geese with their tongues split."

"But I heard you say that you and your family believe in some strange god that has great powers. I heard it repeated that your father was using this great power to force Nimrod to worship your god."

Ori spat emphatically onto the pavement, his lips drawn hard against his teeth. "Lies—lies, they're all lies, and I can prove it to you. Only yesterday I stood here on this tower and heard Nimrod talk with my father as a friend. It is because of my father that we are here instead of down there, like those drowned beasts, in the flood. Nimrod believes in no god, let alone ours. He believes only in himself. Your reason is not strong enough to make prisoners of my family." He repeated the logic of the older men.

Kib felt relieved with this reassurance, but still a question burned in his mind. "Then why—why *were* they taken to the temple?"

"We will find out." Ori turned on his heel toward the center stairway. The son of the king's chief scribe would not yield himself to disclose any reason for his father's disgrace until it be proved, even though he knew the temple guards had been searching for unbelievers.

As the boys descended the stairway to the first terrace the hollow deep-toned rumble of the temple kettle drums sounded suddenly from the temple area. When these great ox-skin drums sounded it meant the heralding of a feast day, or a trial for a runaway slave or for someone caught cheating in business. The voice of the drums could mean many things, but to the frightened boy peering over the wall of the ziggurat, they spoke only disaster for his father.

Led by the call of the drums, the people flowed into the courtyards of the temple and filled the paved terraces surrounding the ziggurat. Beyond the crowds, at the north entrance of the temple, two rows of drummers faced each other awaiting the arrival of the priests. The great paneled doors swung wide and a procession of six priests came out, their shoulders draped in the embroidered robes of state, their waists bare, their lower body covered with tufted skirts of lamb's wool. One priest held the tablets of the law; the other carried the leather pouch in which fresh clay tablets were kept for recording the trial. Behind them came the temple guards, their spears held erect before passive faces. Between them and the next rank of guards came four men, their hands bound behind them, their heads held high.

When Ori saw the faces of his father and Gilgah, hot tears of anger welled in his eyes. Surely this was only a dream—a dream from which he would soon awaken, and he would be back again with Kib fishing in the clear waters of the lagoon. What had happened to make the world so suddenly unreal? Surely Nimrod, if he were here, would not allow the scribe to be harmed. But where was the king? Perhaps Nabu had killed Nimrod so that he could be the king, and now he was using Jared and the others as a cover for his guilt.

Ori's thoughts stopped with the drums. The priests motioned the prisoners to be placed in a row, kneeling, facing them. The records of the law were placed on a low pedestal and the lead priest, raising his hands high above his head, began to speak. Ori and Kib could not hear all the words for they were too far away. They did see, left of the priests, the families of the men, standing motionless, watching the actions of the priests.

One priest after another spoke, each one stepping forward to state his case, each one ending his speech by pointing his hand accusingly at the kneeling men. One of them was robed in the dress of the diviner—those who give the will of the gods. His speech was prolonged with loud wailing cries to the god Enlil, asking forgiveness for the sins of the accused.

When the priests had finished, they beckoned to Ori's mother, and she came reluctantly forward to witness against her husband. Her words were accented with negative shakes of her head and the wide spread of her hands. For a moment she answered proudly—when she spoke of her belief in one God—then finally, under the harassment of the priest's questioning, knelt sobbing to her knees.

Ori could stand no more. Pulling blindly at Kib's arm he ran for the great stairway, tears filling his eyes and blurring the outlines of the tiled steps and the tide of people before him on the terrace below. With Kib close behind, he wedged his way through, until—after what seemed hours—he edged close to the front of the crowd surrounding the trial. Reaching his mother's side, Ori grasped her hand tightly and looked intently into her face. The joy in her eyes met his and left him feeling strong and unafraid.

The lead priest, seeing that the last testimony of the wives had been written, turned to the crowd and called out to a man standing there. Ori recognized the overseer of the brickmakers, the one who had driven the slaves and workmen during the storm. It was the same man that Jared had given the releasement for the workers to bring their families to the tower. He was a powerful man, bearded and broad of shoulder. He walked to the edge of the crowd with a heavy lumbering stride.

"Now you—" the priest pointed to the man, "you, the overseer of brickmaking on the great Etemenanki. Have you ever seen these men bring offerings to our god Enlil or bow before his image?" He pointed to the accused.

The great man shrugged, wary of the position he found himself in. "I follow the instructions of my king. I have no time for making records of those who bow and those who do not bow to Enlil. This is not my duty."

A glint of anger flashed across the eyes of the priest. "But in the line of your duty did you not see the scribe ascend the tower with our lord Nimrod during the storm? Is it not true that when he returned, Nimrod was not with him?"

"Yes, this is true."

"Have you seen Nimrod since then?"

"No, I have not."

"Do you know of any reason why Nimrod did not return with his scribe?"

"We were too busy to think of such things after the scribe returned."

"Why were you busier after the scribe returned than before?"

"He brought us word from Nimrod that we could bring

our families to the tower for safety. When a flood is upon us there is little else to think of."

"And you accepted the scribe's word as authority from Nimrod? Why did the king not tell you this himself?"

"He has many duties. The scribe Jared often brings us commands of the king."

"Did you not think it strange that the message brought by the scribe contradicted the previous orders of Nimrod—that work should continue despite the storm?"

The overseer's brows furrowed as he tried to understand the priest's line of questioning. "Yes, it is strange."

"So," the priest folded his arms across his chest and took a step forward. "You have heard through many mouths that these men—particularly the scribe named Jared—are followers of a strange god. They will not bow before Enlil, the father of all gods, but disobey his ordinances and for this he sent the rains again to swell the flood around us. Now, could not these men also be capable of other crimes? Will you not agree that the scribe Jared—in the devotion to his god—would take advantage of the storm to hinder the work of the tower? That with the magic power of this god he would deliberately destroy the king while they were alone on the tower?"

"That is not true!" Shouting with all his strength Ori sprang forward toward the priest, stopping within a few feet of the scowling face and pointing to the overseer. "The overseer does not know what happened on the tower during the storm, but I do."

There was a murmuring stir among the people as they stretched their necks to see who had spoken. The priests looked at each other, determining whether to recognize a stripling boy who dared to interrupt the priestly court. The leader raised his hand.

"Who speaks with the voice of a young lion, demanding to be heard?"

"I am Orihah, son of Jared the scribe."

"Are you also a believer of the god worshiped by your father?"

Ori did not hesitate. "Yes, I am."

"Then you are not worthy to speak." The priest looked scornfully at the boy. "You are also too young to know truth when you hear it."

Ori bristled. "I am not too young to know that my father saved all our lives. It was he who persuaded the great lord Nimrod to bring the people to safety on the tower. I know this, for I was with them when the words were spoken. I also know that when the king went away to pray in one of the rooms of the ziggurat he was as well as any man."

The priest, seeing that the boy had gone too far, motioned for a guard to take Ori away from in front of the crowd. Then he turned and spoke in darkened tones to his fellow priests. After some agreement they called the diviner forward, who again stood before the people, his hands spread wide in prayer.

"Enlil, whose command is far-reaching, whose word is holy,
  Who perfects the decrees of power, lordship, and
      princeship,
  The earth gods bow down in fear before him,
  The heaven gods humble themselves before him.
  Bring now your wisdom, bring your command concerning
      thy holy laws.
  Speak, O princely one."

With eyes rolled back under flickering lids the diviner stood waiting for the god to answer. Minutes passed as the crowd, motionless and expectant, pressed hands together in prayer. The prisoners, wearied from their cramped positions, shifted the pressure of their bodies from knee to knee. Ori,

48

standing back in the crowd with the guard, felt the grip of the man's hand lessen on his arm.

Fearful of losing ground, the lead priest spoke again, this time directly to the people.

"We must show prince Enlil that we are worthy of his wisdom by favoring the words of his priests. We must acknowledge that those who defy the gods must be punished, for we cannot stand in disfavor before Enlil. He can send more rains and more floods until our city becomes crumbled mud in the river. O people of Babil, you would not have this happen."

A cry of "No, no!" rose from the near listeners.

The priest raised his hands again. "Or, Enlil could withhold the rain so that the drifting clouds will not yield their moisture and the plants and herbs, the glory of the plain, will fail to grow. In field and meadow the rich grain will fail to flower, and the trees not yield their fruit. Surely, O people of this great city, this cannot be."

"No, no, no!" the sound crescendoed into a roar as it issued from mouth to mouth. When the priest could be heard again he shouted, "Then we must punish the offenders." This was instantly answered with the cry, "Yes, yes, punish the offenders!" And the priest, seeing that his words had taken fire, motioned for the drums to begin. The prisoners were rudely jerked to their feet and made to kneel before the praying figure of the diviner. Close behind him, whispering instructions, stood the lead priest.

The drums stopped; the voices of the people were stilled, their ears straining to hear the divine utterance. The hollow, nasal-toned voice of the diviner began.

"O City, washed by much water, filled with steadfast light, dispensing from sunrise to sunset the divine laws to all the people, your heart is unfathomable, profound. The great mountain Enlil in heaven and earth has uttered your exalted

name, so may your divine laws be well directed against those who displease me. . . ."

The voice of the diviner paused momentarily when he felt a tug on his robe from the priest behind him, but in that short silence he heard an unexpected sound which came through the morning air as from the lower regions of the Abyss. His head went up, as a deer who hears the footpad of a lion in the rushes. The lead priest, standing closely behind him, nudged him impatiently to continue; then he too heard the sound.

It was the snorting, splashing noise of moving chariots, coming down the great way through the flood waters of the east gate of the tower walls. This sound did not mean much to any of the other listeners, but to the priests who had been working under the secret direction of Nabu, it meant the disclosure of a private scheme to dishonor the scribe and his family in the eyes of the people. Nabu, rankled by the growing intimacy of the king and his scribe, had used the occasion of the flood, the slaying of the sacrifice, the ensuing rain, and the slave's words telling of the early morning disappearance of the king to rid the court of a man who had become too powerful. If the scribe was not publicly sentenced before the return of the king, the priests would be subject to the fury of a vicious ruler. If the sentence was pronounced and agreed upon by the people, there would be very little that Nimrod could do.

"The sentence—the sentence," the lead priest hissed to the diviner, his voice palsied with fear.

The diviner cleared his throat, and speaking rapidly, shouted out the rest of the message. "All those who have been found unworthy of my favor are directed to be shut from the light of day in the temple prison until they confess their sins. Then they shall be driven from Babil, the holy center of the universe, forever."

Again the drums rolled, and under the sharp commands of the lead priest, the prisoners were hustled to their feet and herded up the steps and through the great doors of the temple.

The crowds murmured their assent to this proclamation of their lord Enlil, and not hearing the oncoming chariots or noticing the weeping of the prisoners' women, turned slowly back toward the tower, thinking now only of their empty stomachs.

Those near the steps of the great stairway heard the shrill cry of an ancient man high above them. He stood, teetering on the top step, his hands extended over them.

"O children of Babil, flee out of the midst of her. Deliver every man his soul, for the Lord of hosts shall fan her and shall empty her land and scatter her people abroad upon all the face of the land unto every quarter of the earth. Hear, O you worshipers of her idols, the days of judgment will come upon her graven images, and she will be cut off. None shall remain, neither man nor beast, from generation to generation, for it shall be desolate forever."

The voice faded away and the birdlike figure disappeared as a mirage before their eyes.

Chapter 6

The Escape

ORI stood close by the temple guard—too stunned to move, too proud to cry, too confused to try to run away. The guard, not knowing what to do with the young prisoner now that the others had gone, looked at the stricken face and spoke gently.

"Great lords do not listen to boys who have sad faces." His eyes looked stern, yet there was a glint of a smile behind them. "If you could lose yourself in the multitude, I think the gods would not disapprove."

Ori gratefully grasped the hand of the guard in a quick motion of trust, then disappeared into the crowd. He wanted to escape from the accusing eyes around him, the echo of the drums, the high whine of the diviners' voice, the memory of his father's disgrace. He worked his way through the crowd moving toward the tower and emerged facing the area of the kilns. Beyond this was the rim of the flood and the outer walls of the ziggurat.

When he skirted the kilns and thrust his feet into the warm, muddy water he saw the great chariot of Nimrod turn from the flooded street into the shallower water of the east gate. A team of four onagers pulled the heavy cart which was loaded with sacks of grain. Nimrod sat on the top, his feet spread wide on the front crossbars, bracing himself against the pull of the donkeys. Behind him, loaded with assortments of melons and fruits, goatskins of wine and oil, palm hearts and dried fish, came other chariots driven by slaves and tradesmen. The wheels of the chariots threw swirls of water as the procession emerged onto dry ground and headed for the court of the temple.

As Ori moved around the kilns, following the chariots, he tried to remember the words of the temple guard. They must have been important, or the memory of them would not be nagging his mind. Suddenly they came to him. The great lord Nimrod would not help him if his face was too sad.

Quickly he ran to overtake the lead chariot. Other boys, seeing the procession, came running. Ori was irritated, for they were ahead of him and had no reason to claim Nimrod's attention. Moving faster, he reached the line of chariots and brushed through the gathering crowd until he came alongside the great cart of the king.

Nimrod was shouting impatiently. He called for his overseer, the temple guards, his scribe, angry that these men were not there to meet him.

Ori called to him, timidly at first, then louder, but the great man was too busy with his own problems to listen to a boy's voice.

Afraid that the temple priests would get to Nimrod first, Ori took a running leap onto the framework between the wheels of the cart and crawled up over the grain sacks behind the king. When the booming voice had stopped for breath, Ori blurted out. "The scribe Jared cannot come to you. He is in prison."

The frame of the king jerked reflexively, then turned slowly on its axis and faced the boy. Wide angry eyes bored into Ori.

"What foolishness do you speak, boy?"

"My father—the scribe—is in prison."

"And why should he be in prison? I have not condemned him." The words were harsh yet filled with concern.

"He defied the gods and brought the rain again." Ori

hurried on. "They said—at the trial—that my father killed you on the tower yesterday."

Unbelief blanched Nimrod's face. "At what trial? There has been no trial. If lies are what you speak, boy, I will have your skin for this."

"The priests tried my father and my uncle Gilgah and two other men early this morning before all the people. They found them guilty! Ask the overseer—he will tell you I speak the truth."

"I smell the odor of priestly rats in the temple." The great man turned his back to the boy. "Go stay with your family where I can get word to you. Now, shoosh, or the cart will be swarming with the likes of you." With this dismissal he shouted again to his overseer who by now was running toward him, followed by an army of attendants.

Ori jumped from the cart. He went to the temple where he had last seen his mother, but he could find her nowhere. Hunger gnawed inside him, and when he looked back and saw the food being unloaded from the chariots and placed in rows upon the pavement, he longed for a morning meal of cheese and barley bread. Remembering the room at the top level of the ziggurat, he quickly sought the little door and, opening it, found the women and his brothers there as he had hoped, sitting around the brazier silently eating. The only bright face among them was that of the Ancient One who looked up smiling as the boy entered.

"Ayee, and here is a boy who has eyes to see and ears to hear bits of truth that are filled with honey sweetness."

"Have you been fishing again," Mahah looked up innocently at his younger brother, "that you have brought us a big fat fish of truth?" He was prone to resent the favors shown Ori by the rest of the family.

"That I have," Ori parried with a thump of his fingers on Mahah's head. "And the fish I caught is six times bigger than you and roars like a lion."

"Come eat your barley meal, Orihah." Mari nodded toward the bowls spread by the pot of steaming cereal. "We have no ears for such light speeches."

"It has the sound of a riddle," Gilgah's wife Timna spoke. "If the fish is six times the size of Mahah, does it have four legs?"

"No, it is not a donkey but sits at the head of a row of donkeys, pulling loads of food, roaring like a lion." Ori giggled.

"That could never be, and you are making foolish jokes, right in the household of sorrow," Mari chided her son.

"But Mother," Ori tried to make her understand, "this fish is the best, for he is going to help us, just as he has helped the people down there by bringing them food. We could have some too, if we wanted."

There was a questioning silence.

"Nimrod?" Timna whispered hopefully.

Ori nodded his head. "We are to stay together until he can get word to us. I talked to him after he drove through the east gate. His chariots were loaded with fruits and grain and oil and melons."

"Where could Nimrod find fruit and grain with the flood spreading as far as eye can see?" Mahah still questioned his brother's reliability.

"Kish perhaps?" Timna suggested. "The city of Kish is along the east branch of the Euphrates. Gilgah has traded there with Gether the miller. He is a descendant of Aram and one of the believers. Nimrod would know him for they are distant cousins."

The Ancient One noisily drank the remaining gruel from his bowl and wiped his mouth on the back of his hand. "It will be a pleasing thing to see Gether again. Before this day is spent we will be breaking bread with him in his house."

"Are you dreaming again, holy father, or is your reasoning affected by the height of the tower?" Mari placed her hand gently on the arm of the old man.

"My daughter, your faith in the wisdom of God has not yet blossomed into full flower. I long to see Gether and his dear family, and you must take me there."

Mari withdrew her hand and stared disbelievingly into space. To be grieved by the loss of her husband, to be accused of faithlessness, and then to be asked to answer the whims of a helpless old man were more than she could bear.

The silence of her bewilderment was broken by the muffled sound of the drums. All who listened dared not breathe for fear of what they meant. Quickly, the younger men of the families slipped through the door, shading their eyes from the sudden sunlight, and cautiously ascended the levels of the great stairway to look down on the courts below.

To the beat of the drums, families came to the rows of food and received their share from the priests. Already little fires made of dried reed stalks and cow dung were blazing under cooking pots on the brick tile of the ziggurat courts. Families huddled to share bits of boiled meat and barley meal, children buried their faces in halves of juicy melons, men grouped together drinking mead and palm wine, while boys and girls munched on crisp cucumbers and palm hearts. The fear of the flood was momentarily forgotten, for the sun was shining, good food was in their hands, and laughter was heard again. The twang of a harp sounded, accompanied by the syncopated beat of the timbrel. Girls began to dance, and soon the whole throng was caught in the abandonment of a festival. Priests, carrying images of various gods, came from the temple. Behind them came the court musicians, playing cithers and reed flutes. Even Nabu, pleased with the success of the morning trial, smiled benevolently at all he passed. A large red bull was driven onto the terrace before the ziggurat and slaughtered for the feast.

Ori, anxious to find Nimrod, broke away from his brothers and worked his way through the people on the stairway past the cooking fires, the dancing girls, and the drinking men, careful not to be seen by any of the priests. A few minutes later he was in the temple stables, surrounded with chariots and onagers which were being cared for by slaves. When asked if they had seen the king, several of the men shook their heads, then one of them nodded toward the passageway leading to the cellars.

The narrow brick pavement felt moist and cool to Ori's feet as he inched his way in the semidarkness to the entrance of the cellars. Cautiously opening the door he looked around the storeroom. It was filled with great jars of oil and wine and sacks of grain, but the king was not there. Down a few steps and to the right was a small door, partially open. He

made for this, but when he opened it he saw only a narrow passageway and darkness.

In the darkness he heard muffled voices, coming from a distance. Then they became more distinct. Torchlight flared suddenly, and Nimrod's scowling face appeared in the passageway. Holding the torch before him, the king came toward Ori.

Ori backed away and ran for the door of the cellar. It would be better to be seen in the outer stables than back in these secret rooms. He had already displeased Nimrod, and a second time that day might be disastrous.

When Nimrod emerged from the hallway, he did not see the boy sitting along the wall for the light of day blinded him momentarily. But Ori was soon by his side, talking rapidly.

"Have you seen my father? Is he in a black prison? Can you set him free?" The words came tumbling out.

Nimrod stopped and soused his torch in a cistern of water before he answered.

"They are in the dark, yes. Their eyes are small as cat slits. But how did you enter the king's stables without being stopped by the guards?"

"I saw no guards. Only the slaves are there with the donkeys. The guards are all at the feast, dancing and singing—even the great priest Nabu. Come, I will show you."

"No . . . no!" The king stared into space for a few seconds. "This may be the time—if your legs are swift enough. Return to your people and bring them here to the stable, one by one. Make certain that none of you are seen by the priests. Now—go to." He gave the boy a sharp slap on his rear and turned his attention to the slaves in the stables.

Ori's heart thundered in his ears as he sped from the spot toward the tower. Much to his relief, his brother and cousins were still together but they were with the family of

59

Lugalbanda. Jacom stood a little apart, talking with the beautiful daughter, oblivious to all around him. The others, laughing and drinking mead, seemed unaware of any need for vigilance. Ori ran at them as a frenzied goose, trying to shoo them back to the tower room. But they held him away, not allowing him to speak. Then Jacom, seeing his young brother's consternation, winked at the beautiful girl and walked a few paces away, ready to listen.

It was not until Ori had explained each detail of his venture in the temple and repeated every word of Nimrod that Jacom sensed the urgency of the moment. He did not understand how his father was to be saved, but he was certain that Nimrod would not lie to them. Even the words of the Ancient One came back, "Before the day be spent, we will break bread with Gether." He looked at the girl, muttering under his breath, "I won't go." Yet he knew he must be with his family, for he was the oldest son and this was where he belonged. He went back to the girl, grasping her arms until she winced, explaining what he must do. She shook her head and clung to him, not wanting to have to make a decision.

Jacom called to his cousins and Mahah, and again the story was told. Their gaiety gave way to solemnity as they looked at their younger brother, then again at the oldest who spoke with such compulsion. Reluctantly they broke away and followed Ori up the steps. Jacom lingered behind with the girl for several moments, then bounded up the steps, leaving her weeping.

The clapping of timbrels, the twittering of the flutes, the chanting, the richness of the food and wine took the people's attention away from those in the procession threading their way down the great stairs. Their backs were laden with bundles of pottery, linens, woolen mats, and baskets of food. An old man was carried on a litter between two young men; a few goats followed the lead of a boy. No one noticed their persistent advance toward the temple except the weeping girl, who walked behind the two young men with the litter, and a boy who came running from the crowd to be with the goatherd.

Kib walked again beside his friend. "You are going somewhere?"

Ori had forgotten all about Kib. Now he felt ashamed, and frightened that he might never see his friend again. "Oh, Kib! I wish you could come with us. But you can't. I know you can't."

"But where are you going?"

"I cannot say, for it is in King Nimrod's mind where we should go. But I think he is finding a way to free my father from the black prison. You must not tell the priests, or they will put a stop to it."

"I would never tell." Kib looked furtively behind him. "But how can you go through the flood?"

"Nimrod is a good king—he knows." Ori pushed on ahead, confident that what he said would be. "And someday I will come back and be the chief scribe of the temple—even to the king, as my father was."

"If I am the king, I will have you. But as long as you do not believe in the gods, the temple priests will not let you. So you had best stay away."

"Yes, I must stay away until all of you believe in One God." In the back of his mind Ori caught a fragment of what the Ancient One had said, that he would go to a land where there were no kings, across the sea. Then he added solemnly as he neared the temple, "And that may be a long, long time."

Quietly the families gathered in the stables under the direction of Nimrod. At the rear entrance two chariots waited, each hitched to a fresh span of onagers. Onto the floor of the carts the families, with their belongings, settled themselves, tense and watchful.

Kib came to the stable entrance, adding ache to pain at

seeing his friend leave him. Behind him the daughter of Lugalbanda came and stood.

It was when Nimrod had disappeared into the passageway to the cellar to bring out the prisoners that two priests, walking unsteadily, came into the stable and stared uncertainly at the scene before them. Their thoughts were intent on the wine cellar and their expressions changed perceptibly as they came to the rear of the chariots and eyed everyone suspiciously.

One waved his arm and spoke sluggishly. "Tukum-bi lu-lu-ra gish-tukul-ta—"

The sound of his unintelligible words stunned everyone who heard him, except the priest who was with him, for he answered without hesitation, "I-la-e"

When Nimrod, with the four light-blinded prisoners behind him, came from the cellar passageway, this priest shouted to him, "Mesheam Iduden?" but Nimrod could not answer. Shouting to the men behind him he rushed the priests. But he too used words unheard by any of the others. Sensing his intent, they seized the priests and tying their hands behind them, pushed them into the storage cellar and bolted the door. When they came into the light again, the bewildered king tried again to speak with his former scribe, but his tongue was clothed with a strange language. Neither of them could speak in farewell except a strong clasp of hands and a quick embrace.

To add another knot to the entanglement of emotions, Milcah, the daughter of Lugalbanda, came running, her long golden hair streaming behind her, her eyes red with tears. She did not stop when she neared the king, but kept her pace until she was on the chariot with Jacom and fell across the packs into his arms. There she clung, sobbing words that no one could understand, as the chariots slowly began to move on through the arch of the doorway into the sunlight.

The confusion of tongues had become a reality.

Chapter 7

The Decision

THE onagers were reluctant to enter the flood waters of the east gate. Jacom, leaving Milcah's side, jumped from the cart and grabbed the bit-ropes of the lead onagers in both hands, pulling the stubborn animals into the water. Gradually they began to move, gaining confidence under the gentle persuasion of the young Babilian who guided them through the dangerous shallows of the flood-washed streets. Gilgah led the second chariot. The other men walked behind, pushing the heavy wooden wheels. Ori looked back to see if they were being followed, but no one came through the east gate—not even Lugalbanda seeking his daughter.

The little procession moved through the streets across the canal bridge and into the shallower road leading south out of the city. The sun was hot, the air sultry. Everyone waded through the muddy water to lighten the load of the chariots. Later in the day the road turned east from the river. It became shallower and finally emerged from the water, deep with slimy mud. Progress was difficult. Arms and legs of the men became smeared with yellow clay as they pushed against the wheels to keep the carts moving through the ruts. Often the men rested, stopping to gaze at the flood behind and the endless trail of mud ahead.

Far along the eastern horizon shimmered the green swells surrounding a distant city. As the day wore on and the road became less muddy, the chariots came nearer and nearer the towering outlines of the palaces and ziggurats of Kish.

Jared turned his cart into a narrow winding street that passed between rows of cone-roofed houses and drove on into the center of the city. It was beyond two large brick silos that he stopped and called to Gilgah; together they walked to the buildings that housed the business of Gether the miller.

Later that night, after the sundown meal, the miller's guest hall was crowded with talking, laughing people. Being of the same family, their language had not been changed. A brazier flared in the center of the room, outlining the faces of the Babilians and the household of Gether. The men clustered near the center, drinking barley broth and chatting together, unmindful of the women and children who formed the outer fringes of the crowd. Jacom and the girl Milcah sat unspeaking in a quiet little island of their own, their backs against the wall. Ori and the other younger boys half listened to the older men, making small jokes among themselves. A son of Gether brought out a hand timbrel. With gentle tapping of his fingers on the skin-covered drum, he began singing one of the ancient songs. Others joined, and soon the room filled with the plaintive music of a wandering people.

When the song was finished, Jared stood among them, raising his hands for silence.

"We praise God that we can breathe the breath of freedom again. That we can here break bread with our friends and loved ones. Yet we grieve that the hatred of men has driven us from our homes and made us aliens among our own people. We cannot stay forever in the house of Gether. If, as the Ancient One has said, we are to go to a strange land, we must decide which direction we should go—east or west, north or south."

Gether spoke. "You are all welcome to stay in Kish as long as you wish. What I have, I share with you. Why go to a strange land? There are many cities along the great rivers. Surely Nabu's priests will not follow you there."

"The risk is too great." Jared swung his body to face the miller. "I am a man of peace, and I am sickened by the stench of idolatry and power-fevered men sweating to destroy each other. Gilgah and I have talked of this often, and we agree that it is better to leave the river cities and return to the open steppes or to the mountains."

"You cannot mean this!" Ethem raised appealing hands. "A man of your learning cannot become a nomad. You are tired. The smell of the dungeon is still in your nostrils."

"Nimrod came from the steppes." Gilgah's voice spoke out. "Is it so strange to believe that we too could establish a new settlement? All of us are skilled in the crafts of building and trade. We do not need to erect another Etemenanki. In some valley among the mountains we could govern ourselves and worship in peace."

"The warlords of Shinar would swallow you in one gulp," Ethem countered.

"Shinar is not the whole universe," Gilgah answered. "There is Assur to the north, Jericho to the west, and the cities of Egypt to the southwest along the Nile. East of Elam, from the cities of the Indus Valley, I have seen beautifully carved lapis lazuli and red carnelian. Beyond the headwaters of the Euphrates comes fine pottery from the city of Hurri. There is space out there for man to find his own brand of freedom."

"But will he be free to worship God? And how desolate it would be!" Gether demurred. "Here we may be in bondage to kings and priests, but we are able to light our torches of knowledge from the fires of their inventions. Surely this is worth something."

"And be seared by the flames of their treachery?" Jared pulled the lobe of his ear nervously. "Truly we are children playing men's games, and we get nowhere. We must decide whether we go east or west, north or south. We cannot stay

65

in Shinar. When the flood waters lower, Nabu will be looking for us."

After a small silence, Omer spoke. "We must seek the wisdom of the Lord."

Others echoed the words, "Yes, we must seek the wisdom of the Lord."

Slowly Jared turned to his brother. "Gilgah, ask the Lord where we should go, then there will be no doubting among us."

Gilgah rubbed his chin with a hardened hand. "The Lord does not always answer our cries with the quickness of spring thunder. But I shall pray for him to speak to us—if it is his will." Shifting his weight upward, he arose and went out into the darkness.

Ori debated whether he should follow his uncle or not. He wanted to share with this man the burden that should be carried by them all. Surely Gilgah would not resent his wanting to help. Quietly he slipped from his place and went out the door.

Bright moonlight cast a yellow glow to the night, highlighting the whitewashed walls of the house and silos, the tiled paving of the outer court. The wild cry of a wolf sounded from the distant hills and Ori, eyes searching through the darkness, saw Gilgah's dark figure walking rapidly away from him down the narrow street. Running swiftly he was soon beside his uncle, keeping pace with the long strides.

"Are you angry with my father?" Ori touched his uncle's arm.

"And why should I be angry with your father?" Gilgah's voice came out of the darkness.

"Because he asks you to do the praying for all of us."

"Is this wrong?"

"It is in my thoughts that we should all do our own praying. I prayed on the tower that I would find my family, and you came along. I know my father prays sometimes, but

66

always when the families are together he asks you to speak for us."

They walked in silence for a few moments. Then Gilgah slipped his arm across the boy's shoulder. "When Jared and I were young, he was the one who took the lead in games, or in tending the flocks, or learning his cuneiform. He could shoot more deer or capture more wild goats than I ever could. He liked people and knew how to be their friends. But the sacred records were my friends—the ancient Book of Remembrance of our ancestors. I spent much time copying its words and discussing their meaning with my father. It was then I learned to pray to the God of the records and the God of my fathers and to listen for his voice. Since then Jared has leaned on me to give the sacred counsel he needed. Often I have helped him; often not. This is a matter of faith— an unwavering belief in things unseen."

Ori's mind captured and held the words he heard, then raced ahead to the prayer yet to be said. "How far must we go?"

"Out to the hills."

"There are wolves in the hills."

"Wolves disturb only those who are cowards." Gilgah looked up at the stars. "I feel closer to God out there on the hills; trying to pull heaven to earth, yearning for my mind to be filled with wisdom."

Ori spoke softly. "Will God speak to you tonight? Will he answer where we should go?"

"If not to my ears, he will speak to my heart." Gilgah looked down at the boy in the moonlight. "Are you afraid of his answer?"

The boy's pace slacked. "As we followed the road today I tried to imagine how it would be to travel where there were no cities, or fields, or homes. I was afraid when I remembered how dirty and tired the traders are when they come from some

67

faraway place." Ori sighed heavily. "I do not want to leave Babil."

"But its prisons are lined with blackness and death," Gilgah added grimly. "We cannot hide our faces from the unknown. We must make it a part of our understanding, then take a trembling step toward it. When we reach the top of the hill, we will be unafraid, for then we can see where we have been."

The man and boy turned from the road and made their way through a small fig grove, then crossed a field to the fringe of hills edging the city. Their bare feet slipped swiftly over the rough ground until they reached the crest of a small hill, tufted with millet grass. In the aura of moonlight, with the blackness of night encircling them, they stood facing the stars and prayed.

The moon edged the horizon in the west, and the cry of the wolves came nearer as the man and boy clasped hands and turned from the place. The boy's spirit sang within him as he felt the joy of the moment, for although he had heard no voice, except that of the night wind, he had felt a divine Presence that warmed him as a cloak and brought peace to his mind. He was no longer afraid of the unknown tomorrow and the unseen lands that lay many moons' journey away. The pressure of his uncle's hand assured him that this indescribable love was shared by them both.

Back at the guesthouse, after Ori had dropped to sleep on a mat by his brothers, Gilgah called Jared to the garden of the outer court; there they talked until the cocks crew and the sky turned pale lemon with morning light.

Once the people of Jared had set their course, they did not look behind but drove their animals and carts northward along the route of the trade caravans which edged the swollen split of the eastern Euphrates. They were leaving the lowlands of Shinar forever. The two brothers strode ahead, their strength affording a shield to their people. The Ancient One was perched on a pile of woolen mats, his frail body jolting and swaying with the cart.

The river lost its swollen anger as the Babilians neared the confluence of its western sister at the village of Sippar. The gardens here held fresh fruits, and the travelers stopped to replenish their food supply and trade bronze bowls for several ewes and a ram. Then they were ferried to the western bank of the river and followed again the route of the trade caravans as it wound northward along the Euphrates.

After days of traveling, Ori walked by the side of his uncle. "How far must we go before we rest?" His legs were tired, and his body was hot.

"We rest when we see the shimmering lake and hear the roar of the lions in the Valley of the Great Hunter. It lies ahead. It is a beautiful spot, dotted with palms and fields of high grasses. Herds of great beasts, tall as a house, come to feed on the tender reed shoots. Wild birds blacken the sky when they are in flight, and the cries of geese fill the whole valley. Many years ago, when we were boys, our tribes hunted here with Nimrod. Since then it has been named for him."

"Is this where we are to stay?"

"It is here I am to have further instruction from the Lord. We will stay until I receive it."

Ori pondered Gilgah's words, then questioned them. "Then where will we go?"

"Into a land which is choice above all the lands of the earth." Gilgah smiled, and the look of blue lakes and great mountains was reflected in his eyes. "And there out of our seed will grow a great nation."

"The land seen by the Ancient One," Ori whispered as he gazed ahead, searching the horizon. Far in the distance, under the heat haze, shimmered a streak of dark green, then blue and gray rolling swells against the sky. Ori pointed toward it excitedly. "Look—there it is—the Valley of the Great Hunter!"

Gilgah squinted under cupped hands. "You are right— it *is* the Valley!" He quickened his pace and called to the other men. The words echoed from mouth to mouth until the whole company, caught in the expectancy of escape from the endlessness of the journey, moved with laughter and singing toward the northwest.

The travelers camped that night in a clearing at the rim of a lake. They made fires of rotted palm wood and dried rushes, against whose embers were placed freshly speared fish and the plucked body of a snared goose. The air hung heavy with the sweet fragrance of pendant clusters of dates and the odors of marsh water and smoke. Old songs were sung, children's laughter rose above the men's talk and the women's chatter as they ate the sweet, hot food of the sundown meal.

After evening prayers, while the red coals of the fires glowed as watching eyes in the darkness, Ori lay on his mat listening to the voices of the night. He could not sleep. A chorus of frogs croaked among the reeds, and a night heron called mournfully in the shallows. From beyond the reeds, another noise caught his attention. It was the splashing and grunting sound of heavy bodies moving into the marshes.

Ori slipped from his mat and, unobserved by the night watch dozing by the fire, ran along the shore of the lake until he neared the fringes of the reedbed. The pale light of a waning moon reflected on the water, outlining huge figures that moved ponderously through the marshes, pulling up the reed shoots and stuffing them into their mouths with long snake-like noses. Ghost-white tusks protruded from their jaws and glistened as the great heads moved back and forth. Ori watched spellbound until one great bull lifted his long snout, sniffed the air, and trumpeted a rasping screech that loosened Ori's feet from the ground and sent him flying back along the lakefront toward camp. Alerted, the herd raised their trunks and sounded their alarm.

The men, hearing the wild cries, were standing with fishing spears poised when Ori came panting among them.

"The great beasts—they are coming!" He spread his arms wide.

Jared reached the boy first, looking intently into the darkness behind him. "How many are there?"

"A great many—more than I could count."

Jared turned to Gilgah and the other men. "We cannot use fishing spears against these monsters. Where can we go that they cannot reach us?"

Gilgah looked at the glowing embers of the campfire. "Fire will frighten them. We can build great flames that will drive them back around the lake—if that is agreed." The men agreed. "Now, go to!"

Quickly the whole camp brought dried reeds and palm branches and pressed them against the living coals. Smoke came slowly, billowed, then sparks of red flame licked upward through the reed torches as they were piled in a great semicircle on the sand facing the camp. The flames rose higher and higher as the thunder of heavy-footed animals came nearer. The bright crackling of the burning reeds and the pungent prevalence of smoke blinded and choked the charging monsters until they trumpeted in terror, then veered from the camp and shuffled away into the darkness.

Jared, red-faced and perspiring, spoke to his little band of defenders.

"If we are to stay in this valley we must fashion spears and arrows of a stout metal that will protect us from such attacks, or our bones will lie bleaching in the sunlight." He looked first at Gilgah's smoke- and dirt-streaked face, then at the others. "Tomorrow those of us who have noses for smelling ore must seek it out, especially if we stay longer than the month of Nisan." He turned to his brother. "How long will we be here?"

"We have only arrived; the Lord has not yet spoken," Gilgah answered. "But there is much to be done, the gathering of goats and sheep, the collection of grains, and the moon of Nisan is on the wane. Surely by seven days we should be on our way."

"But if the Lord does not speak by then?"

Gilgah looked past his brother into the star-flecked sky. "I shall watch by the fire tonight and pray that he will."

Chapter 8

The Cave

A FTER the sunup meal, Gilgah and Ethem divided the older boys between them and set out to explore the borders of the lake in search of food and means of self-defense.

Ori, fearing that he would be left behind, stood half-hidden behind Jacom, a heavy club across his back and a slender bronze knife in his pouch. When Gilgah looked over his little group he saw the stripling there, stretching his height, looking very brave. He gave the boy a nod of approval, and so it was that Ori found himself trotting along behind Jacom and his cousin Pagag, following the giant tracks left by the night raiders.

Beyond the reedbeds and a copse of umbrella-topped acacias, the animal trail led over a barren ridge, then down into the waist-high grasses of a great meadow bordering the lakeside. Deep green trees and lavender hills backed the golden plain, and in the expanse of grass countless herds of animals leisurely grazed.

The hunters stood silent, inhaling the incredible beauty of what they saw. Across the field they identified a band of straight-horned oryx; a few antlered elk; the heavy, long-horned aurochs, cattle of the grassland steppes; herds of onagers; gazelles; and even the monster elephants with gleaming white tusks.

"So it was when I was a boy," Gilgah whispered. "Only now there are more—many more. Surely the lions are all well fed."

Instinctively Ori looked behind him, then stepped closer to Jacom. "If they are well fed, then they will not care to eat us! If a lion comes at me I will beat him on the nose with my club."

"You will be running too fast for that." Jacom grinned. "You stay close to . . ." He hesitated, then stopped speaking when his eyes caught a movement in the low grasses along the lake.

An antelope fawn sprang into view, barely touching the ground as it leaped high through the grasses. Behind it, running in long, sinewy strides, his snarling mouth wide with expectancy, was a huge gray wolf. They came straight toward the group on the swell, but the antelope, seeing the human obstruction in its path, veered abruptly to its left, running toward a thicket of scrub tamarisk facing the swell. The wolf sprang for the kill, missing its mark in a sliding lunge that sprawled it close to the base of the swell. Quickly recovering its balance, the gray form swerved away from the men and made for the thicket.

"Where was your great pounding club?" Gilgah spoke wryly as he looked into the frightened eyes of his young nephew. "No noses will be crushed if you leave it hanging on your back."

Ori said nothing, for his words were tied in little hard bundles inside him.

"Look to the hill above the thicket where the antelope fled." Jacom pointed to the bare, eroded face of the extension of the swell. "There might be flint there for making arrows . . . or bow wood in the trees beyond."

"It is worth a look." Gilgah turned toward the ridge. "And keep a sharp eye for wildcats that might be eager to jump our backs."

74

Ori untied his club and wrapped the thong about his wrist. He would not be caught again without something in his hand to defend himself. He stayed a few paces to the left of Gilgah, his eyes racing over the grasses and thickets for any strange movement there. Then he looked ahead into the tamarisk in search of the wolf and antelope.

From an opening in the taller grasses, he saw another wolf slink into the thicket. A fearful growling and snarling arose, and as Ori and the others followed the sound, they looked down into the craggly branches of the scrub to see the gray wolf dragging the struggling antelope away from the approaching intruder up out of the brush toward the face of the hill. There it disappeared. The second wolf followed cautiously, then stopped, whining—as before a barrier—looking intently ahead.

Gilgah picked a large clod of earth from the rough edging of the hill and, throwing it downward, frightened the second wolf into the underbrush. Looking first in all directions Gilgah waved the others to follow, and they slid down the embankment of the hillside, leaving a trail of dust and rubble behind them. As they neared the bottom they discovered a hollowed cleft in the face of the hill, and in the cleft, the opening to a cave.

Jacom pushed ahead, a large sand rock in his hand. A shout from Gilgah and the sudden fierce snarl of an animal from within made him hesitate.

"We need a torch," Gilgah shouted. "This might be a lion's den."

"It is light enough," Jacom called back. "I can see the wolf from here—over against the wall with her cubs. I see no lions."

The others came up, cautiously looking into the outer chamber of the cave. Half eaten bones were strewn across the cave floor, and over against the wall the wolf stood growling over her kill, her wild eyes staring defiantly. Two fluffy cubs ate ravenously at the torn belly of the fawn.

75

"Look—back in the darkness!" Ori pointed excitedly. "There is a great chamber." His voice trailed off as he slipped along the far edge of the outer cave, away from the wolves, and peered into a great, dimly lighted cavern. Hearing the man-sound, the frightened wolf grabbed her kill in her teeth and dragged it from the cave, her greedy cubs following closely behind her.

Inside the great room the explorers stopped to look about them. Gilgah's foot sank in a dry and dusty ash bed left from the fires of former occupants of the cave. Broken pieces of black and red pottery, with a few stone tools, lay scattered about. Other objects taking shape in the dim light proved to be an assortment of coarsely woven reed baskets, some grinding stones, and several earthen jars filled with grain.

Gilgah kicked about in the rubble of the floor, then picked up a gray-brown stone. "Here is flint." He waved a small ax at Ori. "Go gather tinder and wood for a fire. Then we can see what else is hidden in the darkness."

Moments later a great flame blazed out of the freshly swept firebed. It licked away the dark shadows of the rocky recesses of the walls, disclosing an area that had apparently been occupied by a large nomad tribe. There was space for grinding and storing grains, a tannery for curing animal skins, an area covered with dried grasses and skins, and a corner for making tools and garments.

"What is this grain?" Jacom held up a handful of shiny white kernels he had scooped from an earthen jar. "It is too large for millet or barley seed."

Gilgah thumbed one of the seeds close to the light. "I have never seen such grain before. Surely it will grow, or they would not have harvested it."

"Why are these rocks placed in such a strange way?" Ori stood facing a recess in the cavern wall. "Were they used as a bed or as an altar?"

They all looked and saw a rectangular structure of stones laid the length of a man, protruding half in and half out of the ground. A large stone slab covered the top of the structure and upon it sat a carved stone image of a jackal. Setting aside the image, Jacom and Pagag lifted the flat stone from one end of the rectangle.

"Bring a torch." Jacom motioned to Ori. "We need a light."

Ori caught up a flaming stick and hurried back to the recess. When the group looked down into the open space below, they saw a face, its features modeled in a fine plaster and painted with red ochre. Its eyes stared up at them from smooth round shells placed in the sockets. Around its neck hung several strands of shell and bone beads, including a number of pierced lumps of ore. Pots of dried wheat and millet were grouped about the hairless skull. In one fleshless hand rested a spear, its long, tapered head touching a bony shoulder. In the other hand a long, white tusk, carved with strange cuneiform writing, curved across the bony chest.

"Who is he?" Jacom whispered.

Gilgah studied the figure intently before speaking. "He could be a Guti, from the eastern mountains, or a chief of one of the northwestern tribes. These wanderers drift into the plains during the winter months and feed their flocks along the rivers. But the red paint on his clay face is strange to me—and the beads on his necklace."

"Could they be from the tribes of Canaan?"

"Perhaps. But the jackal image has an Egyptian look, like their god of the dead."

"See the metal spear? It has a strange color—a gray ore like the beads, only this has been refined." Jacom ran a wary finger along the tapered edge. "It is of fine workmanship."

"I have heard traders speak of such a metal. They say that it comes from the mountains of the northwest—an ore that can be heated to a fiery red, hammered into shape, and tempered in cold water. Then it is harder and stronger than bronze."

Pagag looked intently at the spear, then up at his father. "Who needs the spear the most, the dead man or us?"

"Yes," Jacom agreed quickly. "This man's battles have all been fought. He has already slain his wildcats and elephants. With such a fine weapon we could kill larger game for our food."

"We could even kill a lion!" Ori interjected.

"You are not afraid of the curse of the jackal deity?" Gilgah grinned at the boys. "He may howl and snap after you every time you touch the spear."

"I am not afraid of that," Jacom said as he gently pulled the slender shaft from the bony fingers. "This old chief will not object, for his spirit has long since joined his forefathers."

78

He turned back to look at the necklace. "I envy his fine beads, but I fear Milcah would not favor a dead man's jewels for her bridal present."

"You could fashion a ring from the big one." Pagag pointed to one of the larger lumps of ore. "It has a yellow glint to it, more than the others."

Jacom turned the metal between his fingers then slipped it from its sinew fastening. "It will become a beautiful pendant around my bride's neck, for I can carve it with my bow drill." He looked up excitedly as the idea grew in his mind. "With the spear I will bring down my first kill. We can have a feast for the ceremony of joining us as man and wife, and this will be my gift." He gazed earnestly at his uncle. "Can this not be so?"

Gilgah gripped the boy's arm reassuringly. "It can be so."

Calling to Pagag, Jacom ran from the cave, brandishing the spear high above his head and shouting all the great deeds he would perform for the girl he loved.

Gilgah smiled down at Ori, then at the open tomb. "Old Dry Bones should feel pleased that he has brought such happiness to one so deserving. Perhaps we should cover him up before he leaps out to join the wedding feast."

Laughing, the men replaced the cover stones and the jackal head, then shouldering the pots of white grain, Gilgah turned to leave the cave. "Who knows, these seeds may be for Jacom and his bride the finest gift of all."

It was late afternoon when the men and boys returned to camp. Jacom and Pagag each bore a kill across their shoulders. Ethem and his group brought in goose and bustard and strong, slender wood for making bows and arrows. One of the boys had gathered fresh berries and honey from a bee hoard. When Ori and Gilgah laid their jars of grain and two large fish from the lake with the other food, the whole camp, laughing and shouting, came alive with the expectancy of a great feast.

Jacom placed his antelope on a stack of reeds, washed the dirt from his hot face, then sought out Milcah as she sat with his sisters in the shade of a nearby tent. He knelt among the braids of reeds she was weaving, spoke to her quickly, gesturing to make her understand his words, then sat back on his heels to hear her answer. Quietly, with sudden understanding, she looked down at her work, a wave of happiness flushing her face, then nodded her head solemnly. He sped away to find his father and then, with bow drill in hand, disappeared along the lakefront.

While the men were butchering and cutting the meat and the women were building the cooking fires, Ori slipped his fingers into the jar of grain brought from the cave. Clutching a handful in his fist he sought a loamy soil near the lake, scratched it with a stick, and poked the shiny seeds one by one into the ground. After watering the plot, he returned to the camp, fondly imagining what miraculous plant might spring up to surprise the group—and he would be the only one who knew its secret.

The tantalizing aroma of braised meat and brown barley cakes bristling with sesame seeds struck Ori's nostrils as he swaggered past the cooking fires and snatched handfuls of juicy red berries from a fruit-filled platter that centered the eating mats. A young girl, Baba—daughter of Omer—who knelt near the platter, looked up at him reproachfully, for she had taken great care to place the fruits artistically. When he teasingly reached out to smear her face with berry juice she grabbed his arm and clamped her teeth into its flesh.

"You are a cat," he cried, shaking his arm in pain.

"And you are a thief," she retorted, her great brown eyes flashing. "This is the fruit platter set for the wedded ones, and you have spoiled it."

Ori looked at the platter with new eyes, now seeing how the whole effect was damaged by his greed. He looked at the girl again, humbled, but her eyes remained full of hostility.

"I will gather you more—if it pleases you," he ventured impulsively, not considering the cost.

"It pleases me." She rose haughtily and walked away from him. "And it must be soon. The feast time is upon us."

Helpless in the net of his own making, the boy looked around for help, for he was tired and he knew not where the berry bushes grew. None of his cousins were in sight, and the sons of Omer were wrestling in the sand. He wanted to stay and be a part of the last-minute excitement before the wedding. His sisters were going in and out of their tent to twine flowers in Milcah's long golden hair and rub frankincense about her face and shoulders. Timnah had several girls carrying palmyra leaves and fronds from the marshes and red blossoms from the pomegranate trees to decorate the eating mats. As he watched, Ori decided not to get the berries. Girls were not to be obeyed—they were to obey. But while he hesitated, a solemn face with stern black eyes came and gazed at him reproachfully until he turned away and, heavy-footed, sought the path along the lake.

When he returned some time later, empty-handed, for his fear of the lions kept him from penetrating the lakeside thickets, he saw Jacom ahead of him, freshly bathed and dressed in a brightly dyed sheepskin skirt. He was half walking, half trotting to quickly lessen the distance ahead of him. He carried the spear across his back and in his hand hung an object with a long sinew cord.

The sound of the ram's horn echoed across the lake, and drums beat a solemn rhythm in the hot, still air. A bronzed young man stepped from the assembled company toward the tent of his bride. He brought her, flower scented and radiant, into the open shadow of a great palm, where in the smooth sand he laid before her his gifts—horns of his slain antelope, the gray-metaled spear. From his skirt belt a golden pendant was brought, now richly carved; touching her forehead with his lips, Jacom hung it about her neck.

81

Trembling they stood, waiting, as the Ancient One hobbled forward from his palmwood stool to place his gnarled hands upon their bowed heads and ask for them a heavenly blessing. As the last treble whisper of his voice died away, songs of jubilation flowed from the company until it filled the stillness of the valley and stopped the wild beasts in their feeding. Such was the wedding of Jacom and Milcah.

The feast was over, and the sun was a blazing ship riding the lake waters when Jared spoke to his people. "We have been blessed in this valley. The riches of creation are here for us to use with judgment. God wishes us to gather seeds and goats and sheep and cattle for our journeying. He has spoken to Gilgah, and he speaks to us all—to follow his cloud of light. So listen and give heed to his voice. When our preparation is complete, we will follow the trail along the river until it leaves the plain and seeks the mountains of its source. From there the salt air of the sea must strike our nostrils before we rest." He paused and looked at them all. "Are you willing to leave this valley for a road that is strange and hot and long?"

They were silent a moment, then answered as one: "We are willing!"

"So be it!" Jared, relieved with their decision, turned to Jacom. "Tomorrow you are free to do as you wish—to be with your bride. She has given up much to become one with us, her home, her family, her language. The rest of us will capture young animals for the trip ahead. Pagag will carry the spear and protect us from lions or elephants, and young Orihah will take a gathering basket and fill it with juicy red berries."

A laugh rippled through the listeners while Ori, his mouth agape, darted a quick look up and down the row of faces until it settled on the defiant black eyes of Baba.

Chapter 9

Along the River Trail

THE days that followed were strenuous, dangerous ones for Ori.

He first learned to swing a long rope with a noose at the end. By throwing it carefully he caught several young goats and sheep. He was not always so successful. A horned auroch cow saw him throwing his rope toward her calf and started toward him. For several hours he and several other boys chased a band of onager colts until they disappeared into the high grasses. Discouraged and empty-handed they returned to the lakeside.

A stockade was built by the men of the camp to corral the animals they had captured. Ori helped weave strong reed nets which were fastened to the outer trees of an acacia grove. After it was completed the boys rounded up a small herd of cows and calves. By whooping and waving long sticks they maneuvered the wild-eyed animals into the new stockade. A huge old bull tossed his head and bellowed angrily as the herd moved away from him, but the men were able to shoo in the last straggling calf and fasten the stockade gate before he started coming toward them.

The next day, Ori helped separate the calves from their mothers. Several times he had to rush for the safety of a low hanging limb as a cow tossed her horns at him. Gradually he gained the confidence of the calves with tufts of seeded grass and young reeds.

Catching onager colts was more difficult. Time after time Ori and his companions tried to capture wild mares and their colts, but each attempt proved fruitless. They must have more large animals to pull the carts and handle their flocks if they were to reach the sea before the hot summer months began.

One evening Ori, Pagag, and Ethem were coming back to camp from tending the calves. Suddenly they came in sight of a small band of wild donkeys feeding in a clump of grasses near a rocky projection of the ridge wall. There were three mothers and two nursing colts in the group. Giving Pagag one of the long fiber ropes from across his shoulder, Ethem motioned the boys to drop into the grass and move cautiously forward. If they came close enough, silently enough, they could lasso the colts.

Ori, creeping behind, was suddenly attracted to a warm color at the top of the rock ridge. Looking up he saw a lioness

crouching, yellow in the sunlight, sinewy and powerful, ready to spring on the unsuspecting animals below. Fear cramped his throat and, unable to shout or move, he saw the great beast spring forward into the air and land with claws extended and teeth bared onto the back of the nearest mare. A violent struggle followed, intensified by the screams of the fallen onager and the snarling lioness as she sought to break the spinal column.

Ethem and Pagag shot to their feet, paused for a quick look backward, and ran back toward the stockade. Ori finally struggled to his feet and went after them. But as he ran he heard behind him the hard pounding of hoofbeats. He dared not look but cried a warning to the men. Ethem, looking back, unwound his coil of rope and in an instant had the lasso in the air and around the neck of the oncoming onager colt that sped past Ori. Another colt shot into view. Frightened at the sight of the men bending over the struggling animal, it bolted sideways. Not agile enough to make the sharp turn, it fell sprawling before Ori. Moving quickly Ethem shouted to Ori, and together they flung their bodies on the colt, tied its feet, and muzzled the sharp biting teeth. One of the mares trotted along at a distance behind them, whinnying nervously. The third mare had fled.

Pagag handed Ori his spear and left him to guard the second colt while he and Ethem took the first to the stockade. Clutching the long spear tightly in his hand, Ori listened fearfully to the snarling of the feeding lioness, imagining that she had been joined by scores of other lions. The mother onager came closer, sniffing and whinnying, tossing her head up and down in agitation. The colt writhed and strained to loosen the ropes. Ori died a thousand deaths as he waited for the men to return.

Finally they came. Seeing the boy's white face, Pagag gently loosened the spear from the clamped fingers and laid his hand on the trembling shoulders. Ori felt the weight of fear lift from him as he looked into Pagag's smiling face. When the two men bent to sling the onager colt between them, he pranced along behind, the spear extended before him, the hot blood of bravery giving him new strength.

Later, after Ori and the boys had helped tame the colts to be rope-led, the travelers prepared to leave the valley. Tents and skins tanned with the gum of the acacia were loaded into the chariots. Grains gathered from the fields, nuts from the groves, and honey from the tree-hives were stored in reed baskets and earthen jars. Meat cured by the sun was wrapped in palm leaves and packed in cool pots. Tanks made of watertight skins were slung from poles and filled with lake fish.

The last morning before camp broke, Ori took one final look at the shining leaves of the strange reed that had sprouted from the seeds brought from the cave. Selecting the tallest plant, he yanked it from the ground and bore it before him as a banner, wanting the others to know what he had grown. On his way to show it to his mother, he was caught in a herd of goats and sheep pushing their way toward the river trail.

"Move out of the way," called a voice from beyond the herd. "Don't you stand there rooted to the ground. Come help us."

Holding his plant above the heads of the oncoming sheep, Ori looked to the voice. It belonged to Baba. She and her younger brother were working to keep the sheep moving up the slope.

"Who says I must help you?" Ori asked suspiciously.

"Your father and my father both say you are to help us." Baba came closer.

Ori stood deliberating why he, a boy who had helped catch onager colts and hold off lionesses, should be selected to herd sheep with a long-legged girl and her scrawny brother.

"You have tricked me just as you did with the berries. I don't believe you."

"Believe me or not, but ask your father—he will tell you."

The girl's defiant black eyes spotted the green shoot in Ori's hand. "What strange plant is that?"

"I wouldn't tell you if I knew." Ori lowered the plant and hid it behind his back. As he did so, an oncoming goat snatched it from his hand and nibbled it down before he could retrieve the stub of roots from the animal's mouth. He turned angrily at the girl. "Now see what you've done—my very wonderful secret has been eaten." He felt like spitting at her, but knowing the consequences threw the stub to the ground and stomped back to the lake.

"Ori," came the voice of his mother. She was loading the final basket of pottery in the lead chariot. "Ori—come here. Where have you been all this time? You know you have been needed." Slowly Ori came back. "You are to help Baba with the herding. Your father and I felt this would suit you best." She stopped to look directly at her son. "Why are you so angry?"

" 'Tis nothing, Mother." Ori's eyes dropped to his toes, where his heart had sunk. It was true that he would have to herd with Baba.

"Then go to it." Mari pointed to the disappearing woolly backs as the sheep hurried up over the swell.

Stubbornly the boy placed one foot in front of the other, his whole body protesting against the galling prospect of spending the next few weeks—perhaps even months—herding goats with a girl. This would forfeit his being with the older boys when they rode the colts and drove the chariots. After all, he was becoming a man. Did he not stand as tall as Mahah? Were his arms and back not strong as a man's? Did he not help catch the colts and tame them?

The days that followed were repetitious with bright sunlight and southerly winds that blew across the caravan as it moved northwest along the river trail. Broad, shallow depressions gave way to steep, incised valleys where small rivers from the plains cut into the Euphrates. Herds of wild cattle, antelope, and onagers grazing on bunchgrass and flowering rape could be seen along the distant uplands.

One morning Ori drove his small herd onto the trail ahead of Baba's. During the past few days he had been driving alone. By devising a plan that separated his goats from her sheep, he was able to be on the trail ahead of her and not have to join her flock until evening. If she dared to tattle on him, he threatened to scatter her herd. Today, as he watched the purple haze turn to burnished bronze on the hills ahead, he felt the south wind, hot and oppressive, blowing against him. It would be a stifling day. He must hurry the goats over the hills before Baba caught up with him, for he resented her presence during the midday heat when he stopped to rest his goats in the river grasses.

The wind became more persistent, scouring the loose soil from the hard-packed trail and sending it swirling ahead of him. The goats huddled together and, as the wind increased, began to run. Ori looked behind and saw that the horizon had disappeared into a yellowish rolling cloud. Gusts of scorching air rushed by, sending up squalls of blinding dust as the whole sky became overcast.

Suddenly the wind died, bringing a sinister calm. Stopping to regain his bearings, Ori wiped the grit from his eyes and saw that the goats were disappearing into a depression to the right of the trail. It was then that he heard an incredible noise, like the belching of a giant pot of barley meal, issuing from the valley. He broke into a run, fearful for the safety of his goats. As he ran, a sudden gale struck him, enveloping him in a dark sand cloud that stung his body with a thousand minute grits. Struggling through the scudding sands, he descended into the valley, following the dark blotch that was his goats and the belching, sucking sound that grew in awesomeness as he approached. His eyes, stinging with dirt, made out weathered rocky projections along the valley wall. The belching noise deafened his senses to all but fear. Seeking protection from the driving wind, he crouched down behind a ledge to wait out the storm. He spit sand from his mouth, dug sand from his nose and ears, and wiped grit from his burning eyes. The storm continued, tearing at the ledges, tugging at grasses, sweeping every loose object before it.

By the time the wind dropped, a dense yellow layer of dirt covered Ori's body. Shaking himself and brushing sand from his hair, he walked slowly in the direction of the pulsing, gurgling sound. Now that the wind was down he could smell a sulfurous stench which sent a gagging sensation up his throat. Visions of fire-breathing demons hiccuping over his slaughtered goats flashed through his mind as he came closer and closer.

Creeping to the edge of a rough projection he saw below him a boiling pit, throwing gaseous fumes and a black oily substance into the air. Around the outer surface of the boiling mass a solid layer of thick black tar had formed. Edging closer, Ori took his dagger from his pouch and cutting a chunk of the scum fingered it carefully. It looked and smelled like the pitch that was stored in the upper level of Etemenanki which was used to bind the clay bricks together. Gilgah also used such material to make the bottom of his keleks watertight. Wrapping the black square in bunchgrass so he could later show it to Jared, Ori placed it in his pouch and climbed up higher on the ledges to look for his goats.

The air was heavy with yellow fog, but as the wind came again it gradually swept the air clear and Ori could see other belching pits across the valley. He called for Geme but instead of her gentle bleat, Ori saw a group of tall and powerful men step out into the open from between the ledges. They stood looking up at him, their faces masked with dirt, their black hair and beards bushing about their shoulders. They wore close-fitting shirts made of animal hides and carried long, tapering spears across their backs. Behind them moved large, shaggy-haired animals Ori had never seen before. They were built much as the onager but were broader-backed, smaller-eared, and fuller-faced, with long flowing manes and tails.

The men came closer to the base of the ledge, eyeing Ori suspiciously. One of them, pointing toward the trail, spoke. Ori opened his mouth to answer, but not knowing what had been asked—as the language was strange—he pointed toward the valley and stammered: "I was looking for my goats."

Following Ori's direction with their eyes, the men noisily jabbered with each other for a few seconds, then at the command of the leader, one of them trotted off through the ledges. In a few minutes he returned, driving Geme and the other goats before him. Ori breathed freer now. These people were his friends—they were, like him, hiding from the storm—probably lost and hungry. Calling to them, he jumped from the ledge and waving toward the trail, rounded up his goats and began the climb out of the valley. The men and animals followed, and soon they were up on the sand-scrubbed trail. Looking southward, Ori saw the wind-battered caravan creeping toward him, Baba's sheep in the lead. She had evidently not started before the storm struck. Her eyes would really open when she saw him bringing in such powerful friends. Her mouth would drop open like a baaing sheep when she saw . . .

Ori's thoughts were suddenly shattered when he felt himself grabbed from behind by one of the men. Before he knew what was happening he was hoisted into the air onto the shaggy back of one of the animals. A strong-faced man with a prominent nose jumped on behind, holding Ori tight against his body with one arm while he guided the animal with the other. The whole group mounted, and waving their spears over their heads, howling blood-chilling cries, they swept down the trail and swarmed about the unprotected caravan.

Baba's eyes were wide when she looked up into Ori's frightened face. He was not a hero now, with a long shining dagger at his throat as the man behind him shouted threats to the men driving the chariots.

Getting no response from the caravan men, who did not understand what was being demanded, the man waved orders to his companions. Dismounting, two of them attacked the lead chariot, dumping tents, bedding, pots, sacks of grain, and dried food in wild profusion over the ground. Not finding what they sought, they pounced on the second chariot only to come face-to-face with the Ancient One cradled on a pile of tenting. Behind him crouched Milcah, protecting his wind-burned eyes with a large reed fan. As they grabbed the old man's arms to jerk him from the cart, he spoke to them quietly in their own dialect.

"Are the eyes of the followers of the god Amurru so blinded with sand that they cannot see that their greed is wasted on this wretched procession?"

The men loosed their hold on him, their eyes narrowed with apprehension. "You are from that great city of Babil," one man answered. "All those who come from Babil are rich with gold and silver ornaments."

"As you see, we are not laden with riches of gold and silver." The Ancient One spread his hands. "But we do have an abundance of sand to which you are welcome."

"You betray us with lies—you crow." The second man spit through his teeth for he was looking at the pendant around Milcah's neck. His fingers reached out and broke the ornament from its cord. He did not anticipate the fury unleased as the frightened girl sprang to retrieve her loss. Scratching and biting his offensive hands, she dug the pendant from his fingers and struggled backwards across the body of the old man to the upper reaches of the cart, the pendant clutched triumphantly in her fists.

With a roar of rage the man went after her, climbing over the Ancient One and reaching out dirt-encrusted arms to drag her from the cart. But as he pulled her toward him, a long, steel-pointed spear pressed at his throat. He slowly relinquished his hold on the girl as looked up into Jacom's grim face.

An excited chattering erupted between the two men when they saw the extended spear. The lead man, relaxing his dagger hold on Ori, rode forward, his eyes fixed on the glittering blade, his face a mask of unbelief.

"What are they saying—why do they stare so?" Jacom whispered hoarsely to the Ancient One.

"They speak of one Dagan, a great chieftain of their tribe who carried such a spear."

"Why do they think it is the same spear?"

The Ancient One straightened to a sitting position and spoke to the man holding Ori. "Could not such a spear be made in the great city of Babil?"

The leader shot the old man an insulting look. "Only the god Amurru knows the secret of forging such metal. Only Amurru, whose power lies in the silver mountains of the north. This was his gift to Dagan, the mighty chief of our people. Dagan left to battle the tribes of Assur to the east many, many moons ago." The man sat frowning as he looked at Jacom, then eyes ablaze, bellowed out, "You are one of the evil jackals of the east. You have killed Dagan and taken his spear. For this I will split you end from end." He moved threateningly toward Jacom.

"Harm the boy and you will be struck down by the anger of Amurru," the Ancient One warned. "Are you greater than Dagan that you would defy his will?"

"What riddles are you saying?" The piercing eyes bored into the old man.

"I'm saying that Dagan gave the spear to Jacom, our son, for the protection of his people. Even the golden ornament, torn from the girl, came from the silver mountains. These were marriage gifts—gifts of the gods of high places—from Dagan to these our children."

The dark strangers stood silent, not wanting to believe, yet not daring to disbelieve. Then, devising a face-saving decision, the leader pulled the head of his animal toward the trail, took a fast hold on Ori, and motioning to his men, rode away shouting, "Dagan did not give you this stripling. He will become a slave to our women."

Chapter 10

Captivity

FOR six days Ori rode behind his captor, following the trade route to the west as it wound through the monotonous hills and flats along the river. At every marsh or grove, the riders stopped to search the herds of wild game for some animal they could not find, for they left the others untouched. Ori listened to their incessant chatter, feeling their keen eyes watching him for any attempt to escape.

On the sixth day they rode into a sprawling settlement that hugged the hills south of the river. A number of dark-skinned women and children, wearing brightly colored dresses, swarmed out from the mud huts and tents to meet them. They uttered inarticulate sounds—happy talk that sent a wave of homesickness over Ori.

He slipped to the ground, unnoticed, and stood watching the exchange of affection between the men and their families. A tinge of remorse swept his thoughts as he considered again how his foolishness had brought him to this place. If he had not been so intent on evading Baba he would now be sharing the sundown meal with his own family.

A friendly dog came up, wagging its tail. Then a curious child with wide black eyes looked at him intently. From among the women came a slender, sure-footed girl, older than Baba, with blue and green patterns in her dress and long, flowing hair. She beckoned to Ori, and moving swiftly to a conical shaped tent opened the flap for him to enter.

Inside were several older women, sitting on skin mats grinding wheat into flour with stone mortars. They looked at him critically, appraising his sand-brown skin, his dirt-caked face, his tired, sagging shoulders. One old crone, perhaps the mother of them all, spoke to the girl, then apparently forgetting he existed went back to her grinding.

The girl took Ori to a sunken, spring-fed pool in a rocky recess off the hillside. She stripped off his woolen skirt and began pouring cool water over his grimy body. Then she scrubbed his hair and skin with a rough, oily soap, tossed him a long, coarse cloak, and led him to a tent lined with animal skins. She brought him a bowl of dried meat and thick pea soup, then left him alone.

It was much as if he had not eaten or slept exhausted, for with the light of morning he saw the girl again, standing over him, pulling him to his feet and out into the chill morning air. The villagers were astir—building breakfast fires, feeding the animals, milking the goats. After being fed fresh goat milk and wheat cakes, Ori was brought before the old woman again for instructions. A stone adze was thrust into his hands, and he was motioned to follow a group of women and girls into the fields bordering the river.

All day he worked among the women; filling the irrigation ditches, hoeing the melons, winnowing the ripened winter wheat with large wooden forks. When sundown came, his aching back and blistered hands welcomed the sight of the village compound where there was rest, food, and the drug of sleep.

The second day went much as the first, but before he went to the fields a small round circle was burned into the skin of his left shoulder. It was the brand of slavery.

After the midday rest on the third day the women looked up from their work, and pointing up the river began chattering excitedly.

Following their eyes, Ori saw a string of rafts drifting slowly with the river, the helmsmen with long oars appearing as diminutive flies on straw bundles. As they drew nearer, several of the younger women ran back to alert the villagers. Men, women, and children soon gathered along the riverbank, talking and shouting, some running along the water's edge, others standing with folded arms, waiting.

Slowly the rafts, guided by the long poles of the oarsmen, left the main current of the river and edged into the drift water along the embankment. Throwing out anchor lines, the men scrambled ashore, secured the rafts, and then moved with the villagers up the incline through the fields to the settlement. Two of the rivermen carried a great wooden box across their shoulders.

Ori stood behind, undecided as to whether he should stay in the field or follow the others. No one seemed to care or look in his direction, for their attention was with the strangers and their great wooden box. Even the girl who had kept watch over him was gone.

The idea of escape fastened itself in Ori's mind. He could run east down the river, hiding in the folds of the hills, then follow the trail back to his people. Even if the men, with their fast-riding animals, came after him, he could flatten himself among the grasses.

Cautiously he laid down his adze, looked back again toward the village, then slipped over the ridge above the river and began to descend the slope. It was then that he noticed a man sitting with his back to the timbers of the second barge, his head tilted back, as a fine stream of red wine poured from a clay jug into his mouth.

Ori stopped, fearful that the man might cry out when he saw him, but as he looked at the man, his coloring and dress, he recognized a native of the lower rivers—a man from Babil. Eager to speak with one of his kind, Ori half ran and half slid down the rough surface of the

incline until he came to the leveled sand edging the river. The man on the raft eyed him suspiciously, shoving the jug of wine out of sight as Ori drew nearer. As the boy started to board the raft, the oarsman shouted at him, waving him off the raft. At first Ori could not understand what the man said, but soon he recognized the words of his own language.

"Are you from the city of Babil?" Ori asked slowly, then repeated it. "Are you from Babil?"

The man's eyes narrowed. "Babil? Babil?" He wiped his wine-stained mouth with the back of his hand and nodded his head. "Babil . . . home." He pointed toward the village, then to Ori. "Why . . . you here? . . . Amorites?"

Ori thought he understood. "I am their slave. They

took me from my family three days ago—back along the trail." He pointed to the east.

The man nodded knowingly. "Your father trader?"

Ori shook his head. "No—no—scr . . ." Then he remembered the danger he might bring to his father if he told this man who his father was. "We go to find a new home—to the west—to the great sea."

The man squinted one eye against the sun and pulled the jug from behind him again. ". . . . good to leave . . . prison of Nimrod. I am his slave . . . I bring cedar . . . oak . . . palace." He took a long, breathless swallow from the jug.

Ori was quick to correct what he thought the man said. "Nimrod is not building a palace. He is building the great tower, Etemenanki."

The oarsman leered at Ori. "Nimrod . . . palace . . . cedar walls . . . ivory ornaments, lapis lazuli . . . silver. Amorite hunters . . . kill elephant herds . . . trade for copper . . . Egypt. Horses carry tusks. . . ." He measured with his arms the length of that of which he spoke.

"What is a horse?" Ori wanted to know. He had never heard the word before.

"Horse?" The oarsman laughed. "Not know horse . . . Babil. Amorite . . . east of silver mountains . . . run fast . . . carry man . . . broken." The man crawled over on his hands and knees, tossed his head, and pawed the floor of the raft with his hand.

"With a horse I could find my people." Ori glanced back toward the village.

The oarsman looked intently at Ori then shook his head. "Amorite kill for horse—you run away . . . own legs."

"My legs won't run fast enough. I might be caught—brought back here to be flogged—or killed."

"Run now—go." The oarsman sat back on his heels. "Amorites come back . . . soon." He jumped up from his crouched position and pulled Ori off the raft onto the shore.

97

With his finger he traced lines in the wet sand. "Go south Amorite . . . on to mountains . . . Lebanon . . . forests . . . to great sea." He waved for Ori to go south along the riverbanks away from the village.

Ori looked back up the incline. No one was in sight. As he turned to leave the river's edge, he caught a glimpse of someone standing on the ridge above him. It was the girl who had watched over him the past three days. She was waving to him—calling for him to come.

Ori broke into a run. He would outwit the girl and be far down the river by the time she could run for help. She did not turn back as he anticipated, but kept him in sight, dodging along the ridge above him. He stumbled over rough rock outcroppings, slid on loose gravel, and once fell to his knees, but she was always behind him.

Coming to a ravine, Ori ran under cover of its banks away from the river until it narrowed into a thicket of grasses. Flattening himself he lay panting, his body exhausted, his heart pounding in his ears. He would wait to see what the girl would do. Even if she found him he was certain she could not force him back to the village. It was hard for him to imagine that her eyes could grow cold and hard, her voice sharp and demanding, for she had always been gentle—almost motherly—to him.

When Ori finally raised his head to look behind him he saw only the tall grasses and the rise and fall of the swells. Perhaps the girl had given up the hunt and returned to the village. Above the noises of the wind came the sound of someone speaking. Ori strained upward, fearful of being seen, yet curious to see, for the voices came from men and the men could be Amorites.

Peering through the thicket ahead of him, Ori stared in unbelief, for coming toward him over a rising swell, their faces squinting against the sun, were Jacom and Pagag.

Bursting from the thicket, yelling incoherently, the boy

ran to meet them, sobbing with happiness. They came toward him, folding him into their concern, turning with him back to the south where the trail lay.

They had gone only a short distance when a woman's cry came from behind them. It was the Amorite girl, running and calling to them, her face and voice fearful of them as men, yet seeking their understanding as human beings.

"What is she saying—what does she want?" Jacom spoke to Ori.

"She came after me when I ran away from the river raft. It was in my mind that she wanted to take me back—to keep me a slave." The boy paused. "They did make me a slave—see!" He turned his back to show the round encrusted burn on his shoulder.

The girl, seeing the scar, came closer, chattering rapidly. She motioned to herself, then to them. She turned her back and pulling away her garment, showed an identical circle on her own shoulder.

"She's a slave!" Ori shouted. "She wants to be one of us."

Gesturing for them to follow, the girl ran away from them toward the trail, pointing in fear toward the village. Following the direction of her pointed finger, they saw a cloud of dust rising above the confines of the distant settlement. The men had returned from the hunt!

Haste nipped at their heels. It was not until the sun had slipped low in the afternoon sky that the caravan came into sight. After the four had eaten and rested, a council was held. It was decided that the migration would follow the route suggested by the oarsman. It would leave the river trail and go directly west, away from the Amorite village, toward the Great Sea. Water casks and skins were filled, and the procession began, following the ravine out of sight of the trail. When nightfall came and stars dotted the evening sky, the company did not rest but kept to the course of the valley. Finally, when night reached its zenith, they paused.

Long before dawn Ori was awakened. Groping through the darkness he joined the other members of his family in rounding up the livestock. They must lengthen the distance between them and the hunters. All that day they faced the west. When the afternoon heat forced them into the shadows of a sheltering hill, Ori and Pagag climbed its summit to scan the northern horizon for possible pursuers. Far to the east they saw a band of wild donkeys trying to escape two horsemen armed with bows and arrows. The group bore northward, finally disappearing over a swell. A low, dense cloud of dust rolled with the wind behind them, obliterating the horizon and filling the sky with choking yellow dust.

Ori felt relieved. They were safe at least until the wind subsided. As the ravines and hills stretched out before them, he kept a constant lookout for roving bands of tribesmen and wild animals at the waterholes.

One day, when they moved through a narrow passageway between two ridges, a great black-maned lion roared out from his rocky shelter ahead of the caravan and pounced on one of the lead goats. Jacom, only a short distance behind, lowered his spear and moved cautiously toward the beast which was hungrily mangling the body of the ewe. Seeing the man coming at him, the lion backed away from his kill, snarling and lashing his ribs with his tail. As he crouched to spring, Jacom's spear shot forward and pierced the shaggy neck, close to the shoulder. The wild glaring eyes lost their luster; the great dripping mouth sagged as the body heaved forward in death.

In the days that followed, Ori herded his goats ahead of the caravan watching for water sites. Their water supply was almost gone. Small shining pools seen in the distance proved to be milky shallows encrusted with salt. What once had been spring-fed streams were now dry beds shriveled with the sun.

One day Ori saw a small lake on the horizon. Shouting to the others he ran to taste of its sweetness, but when he neared the palm-fringed shore he saw, sprawled among the trees, a great tribal encampment. Surrounding the lake were hundreds of sheep and goats; men, women, and children, dressed in long tunics, moved within the complex of goatskin tents.

Ori turned back and quickly directed the disappointed travelers in a wide half-circle away from the lake into the shelter of the hills. His people moistened their parched lips with the remaining drops of water and kept their pace toward the setting sun.

The next day dark clouds swept across the western sky, dumping a torrential downpour over the trail. The people turned their heads upward, grateful to feel the life-giving water beat against their dust-covered bodies and wet their thirsty throats.

The caravan now moved westward through ragged hills backed by the outlines of distant mountains. Spring-fed streams trickling through the sandstone projections of the hillsides exposed lumps of bright metal. The Babilian men came, fingering and nodding over the feel and color of the golden ore. They stayed their march while they searched the streams and sands for the precious metal. They placed it in a large clay crucible where it was melted with silver and copper and made into yellow gold. When it had cooled enough, Jared hammered it into thin sheets. On these, with a bronze-tipped stylus, he wrote in fine, detailed cuneiform the record of their flight.

After crossing a broad river valley lush with tall grasses and wild grains the travelers saw that beyond the foothills a great range of mountains formed a massive barrier ahead of them. Milk-white crests, circled with clouds and sunlight, towered above the silvery gray limestone of their slopes and the deep green of their forests. It was a beautiful but foreboding sight, for it separated the Babilians from the Great Sea.

But as the caravan moved into the mountains, it came upon a great valley slashed from the massif range, a valley of steep cliffs and rugged gorges, opening up a passageway to the west. Carefully the travelers threaded their way through the twisted strata of colorful lime and sandstone of the rift. Here among the rocks they found deposits of dark ore resembling that of the Amorite spear. They smelted this in a small rude furnace and, after tiring experimentations, fashioned spears, arrowheads, and knives from the metal. It was strong and durable, harder than bronze, and could be sharpened and hammered into many shapes. There would be no fear now of attacking lions, for all the men were well armed.

It was when the caravan emerged from the depths of the rift, up through the maze of shrubs and forest growth, and climbed to the crest of the fault that they saw—far to the western horizon—the haze-blue of the sky merge with the indigo of the Great Sea.

Chapter 11

The Great Sea

ORI and Mahah, sun-bronzed and toughened by the wilderness journey, marched ahead of the caravan, herding a small band of goats through towering cedars and pine down the western slope of the mountains. They scuffed through beds of yellow-horned poppies, passed over snow-fed streams, and pushed their herd toward a break in the forest ceiling where the trees thinned and the blue sky broke through.

Down the long slope to the south, Ori heard the unexpected sound of men's voices shouting. Running quickly to higher ground he saw below him a procession of ox teams straining to pull a load of pine and cedar logs across a rocky ravine. Around the oxen, shouting and cracking long snake whips, worked copperskinned drivers, harassing the beasts forward up the slight incline.

Motioning to Mahah, Ori circled the goats and herded them out of sight of the drivers. He had learned, since his captivity, to trust no stranger. These men could be enemies as easily as they could be friends.

"There could be a city close by," Ori conjectured. "The oarsman on the river said there were cities along the rim of the sea. These men might capture us and take us to the city without Father knowing it."

Mahah pressed his palms to his hips and spat into the wind. "They will not bother us. They are probably slaves for the Egyptians and would not give us a second look. If they do, we can hide before they reach us. You are too much like a rabbit." Mahah looked through the trees to the distant horizon. "I would like to be in a city again. To see streets lined with markets and strange people. To live in a house and sleep in a comfortable bed." He sighed heavily. "Let's follow the men. They need not see us, and perhaps over the next slope we can see the city and the coastline."

Ori hesitated, then moved with his brother, away from the ox teams, to the hill ahead. Surely if they were careful not to show themselves there would be small harm in exploring the land beyond them.

As the boys edged along the rim of the next incline they came suddenly onto an isolated shrine. Crowning the hill was a rectangular shaped stone temple, its high open door facing the east. Around its court was a circular fence of man-high pillars made of wood and stone, some needle-pointed, others blunt and square. Before it stood a stone altar, stark and bleached in the sun. The boys crept closer to the shrine until they could see into the court facing the temple.

In the distance they heard the muted tones of a drum and the rhythmic wailing of a chant. The sound came closer and closer. Then a long line of men and women came into view, threading their way up the hillside into the temple area, waving flags dyed with brilliant purple and scarlet. Draping the flags over the pillars, the worshipers knelt facing the entrance of the temple.

"They are worshiping their gods—just as the people did in Babil," Ori whispered. "I wonder if their god is Enlil."

Mahah frowned and put his fingers to his lips. "Listen—don't speak."

Presently a priest, dressed in a fringed scarlet skirt, his head crowned with a pointed helmet, came out of the temple and stood before the door, holding high a crudely carved

image. When the worshipers saw the hollow-eyed wooden god
they cried out, pounding their chests and pulling their hair
in a frenzy of adoration. Another priest appeared at the door.
He carried a long, razor-sharp knife, and holding it before him,
stepped forward and began shaving the heads of all those who
knelt in the circle surrounding the altar. As the long strands
of hair fell from the women's heads, they whimpered little
cries of distress. When their heads shone bald in the sunlight
they moaned as they rocked back and forth on their knees,
their faces hidden in cupped hands. When the shaving was
completed, the incense bowls were lit. Whorls of smoke rose
with the wind, giving off a spicy fragrance into the air. The
second priest brought a snake from a nearby pit. He held it
high over his head as he chanted, then wound its glistening
body around the statue of the god. He repeated the word

105

"baal" over and over in the chant. The people's bodies swayed as in a trance before the snake.

Ori barely breathed. As he watched he noticed a small group of people at the far end of the circle. A young man and woman were holding a small baby wrapped in purple linen. They knelt without praying, their heads bowed over the tiny infant. Behind them were clustered members of the family—mother and father, brothers and sisters, all silently kneeling, paying little attention to the chanting priests.

Suddenly the drums began an excited rhythm. The first priest, followed by a group of chanting singers, circled the altar. Resting the god image on one end of the great stone, the priest turned to the group Ori had been watching and called to them. The young father stood, holding the tiny baby tightly in his arms. He hesitated momentarily, then slowly placed one foot forward, then another, until he breached the gap separating him from the altar. He tenderly placed the baby on the sun-warmed stone and stepped backward a few paces, waiting, his face drawn tight.

Watching closely, Ori drew in his breath sharply as he saw the priest with the razor step from behind the idol and, unwinding the linen swaddling clothes from around the small olive-skinned baby, slash its throat. It was just as he had remembered the sacrificial goat at the altar of Etemenanki. A chill shook his body as he heard the young mother scream and faint into the arms of her family. He watched the priest rewrap the baby in the bloodstained linen, saw him place it head first in a tapered jar and cover it with a clay bowl. The jar was carried to a corner of the temple and lowered into a hole where it was covered with a thick flat stone.

The gruesomeness of the ritual sickened Ori. He turned away and edged his body back through the shrubs out of sight of the temple. Mahah followed him, and together they silently crept back toward their flocks. Ori stopped once to look back. He saw the family of the baby trailing down the slope behind them, a lonely procession of grief. Sympathy choked his throat when he looked at the young mother. As the group came closer tears ran unchecked down his cheeks.

Sudden anger welled up inside the boy—anger at the priest and all the chanting worshipers who willingly allowed one of their own children to be killed as a sacrifice—just like an animal. Not one of them raised a hand in protest or spoke out against it. Were they afraid of the priests—the snake—the gods they worshiped? Would they have better crops—would the rains fall more often on the fields? If only he could tell these people of his God. Anu was a God of life, not of death.

Gathering his courage, Ori spoke a soft "Peace be with you" as the last of the straggling group passed by him.

A tall, broad-shouldered man stopped and bent his gray head toward Ori. His face was kind and he smiled quickly; then he spoke. Ori could not understand what he said. It was a language he had never heard before.

"Come along, Ori," Mahah called. "These are strange people. Father will be angry if you are captured again."

"This man would not hurt me," Ori protested. He would not give up so easily. "We must help them—tell them of our Anu." He looked back at the man who had turned to follow the group.

"They would never believe in Anu," Mahah shouted. "They can't even understand you. Leave them alone." His voice commanded Ori to obey him.

Still Ori hesitated. He looked beyond Mahah and the grazing goats and saw the caravan threading its antlike way down the forest slope toward them. Gilgah and Jared were in the lead with the cart of the Ancient One close behind. The Ancient One—he could speak the strange language of the tall man.

Ori ran shouting after the family group, trying to attract the tall man's attention. Hearing the boy's voice, the stranger stopped and turned. He looked at Ori, then up the slope where the boy was pointing. He saw the caravan, the men with spears, and shouted for his family to run, but Ori kept after him, pulling on his sleeve until he stopped, willing to take a chance because of the concern in the boy's face. Ori urged him back up the slope, to the crest of the lower hill were Mahah stood, and they waited for the men of the caravan.

Ori shouted his story in short, breathless sentences, eager to see if Gilgah or the Ancient One or his father could understand the tall man's words. It was the Ancient One who tried phrases in first one dialect then another until he hit upon one the stranger understood. They talked excitedly as their understanding grew, until finally the Ancient One turned to Gilgah and Jared.

"He is an Egyptian shipbuilder from the city of Gubla. He and his sons live at the shipyards along the Great Sea—not too far from here." His bony finger pointed westward over the low hills. "He is a slave to the princes of Gubla. He tells me that we too will be slaves if we are caught by the guards. We could be taken to the Egyptian copper mines at Sinai, far to the south, or kept here in the mountains hauling timbers for the ships. He will shelter us until sunrise. After that it will not be safe."

Within the hour the caravan moved to join the huddled family of Sephar the shipbuilder. Together they walked smiling but unspeaking away from the fringe of the forest, over the rolling hills into the coastal plain, following the valleys and ravines away from the sharp eyes of Egyptian hirelings. Near sundown they came in sight of the sea, stretching from deep purple to brilliant orange in the sunlight. They ate their sundown meal inside the walls surrounding the adjoining houses of the shipbuilder's family.

Ori and Mahah, excited to be near this much water, left the house to investigate the harbor.

Yellow light reflected on the rippling waters lapping the rough stone pier that jutted from the rocky shore. Cedar logs, hewn from the upper forests, were cut and stacked in crisscrossed piles about the harbor, ready to be shaped into ship's timbers. Two long, graceful barges lay alongside the pier, their single two-legged masts supporting beams for one square sail. Tapered vertical prows projected high above the top of the pier. Smaller reed boats bobbed on the water at the pier's end. They were longer and narrower than keleks with prows bent upward, their sides and bottoms coated with a heavy resin.

As the brothers made their way back to the house of Sephar, Ori almost stepped on a spider-like object crawling along ahead of him. It had long spindly legs with two projecting claws that waved above it as it raced sideways toward the piles of timber. Ori forgot Mahah in his anxiety to catch the strange creature. He dodged this way and that as the crab changed course. He never took his eyes from it until the crab ran over the extended foot of an Egyptian workman who sat crouched with his fellows among the ship's timbers, drinking wine from a long, tapered jar. The men looked up in surprise, not used to seeing strange-faced boys coming upon them so unexpectedly. Anger replaced the startled looks, and quickly laying aside the wine jar one man sprang to his feet and made a lunge at Ori.

Shouting a warning to Mahah, Ori turned sideways, imitating the course of the crab and dodged through scaffolding and timbers. He dared not run to the house or the whole family would be captured. Mahah did not answer his cry.

Desperate to escape the long-armed Egyptians, Ori slipped into the water among the rocks and swam underwater toward the pier. After taking what seemed like the longest breath of his life, he surfaced close to the stern of the farthest barge and found himself facing the sunset. Treading water, he clung to the timbers of the boat, fearful that any minute someone would come along the pier looking for him. He could hear the strange words shouted along the shore, and he lay with only nose and forehead protruding from the water until the voices died away. The sun sank, and Ori cautiously swam back among the reed boats. He crawled over the edge of one and flattened himself exhausted against its water-soaked bottom.

He wondered if Mahah had been caught by the Egyptians, if anyone had asked why he was not in the house of Sephar . . . if . . . His eyelids drooped, and as he tried to reason his mind drifted into a dream of strange faces peering at him, faces grotesque in color and expression—some with long hair and painted beards, others with round, shaven heads, others with great open mouth, calling him in whispered tones with plaintive little shrieks like cries of wild geese flying in the marshes. They grew louder and more distinct, their images pressing down upon him, the shapes of their faces merging with long, hooked noses and no eyes.

With a little cry of horror, Ori thrust himself upward out of the boat into semidarkness. There were voices around him—soft stealthy voices—but they had a familiar sound, a Babilian sound. As he listened he picked out the voice of his father and Sephar the shipbuilder. In the rise of the night wind he heard the shuffling movement of sandaled feet on the surface of the pier, then the sharp accent of small animal hooves, the heavier thud of bigger animals, the brushing of bodies and burdens against each other.

Unfastening the mooring rope and grasping the attached oars of the reed boat, Ori edged it away from the end of the pier and pushed it toward the barge. It was difficult to steer through the water in a straight course.

As the sound of the oars came across the water, the voice of Sephar called out a hushed command in Egyptian.

Ori realized then that they did not know who he was. "I am not an Egyptian," he cried hoarsely. "I am Orihah!"

Then Jared's voice came clear and strong. "Come quickly, my son. We were about to leave you behind."

Ori's arms ached as he pushed against the oars, first on one side, then on the other until the long reed vessel came head on into the side of the barge. Throwing the mooring rope up to the waiting men, Ori scrambled out and aboard the hull of the barge, landing feet first in a huddle of woolly animals. Clinging to the rail of the bow he edged away from the hot, smelly bodies toward a cluster of women and children, their mounds of belongings piled around them.

As he came into the group, two strong arms reached out and pulled him close. In the next few startled instants he recognized the presence of his mother. Her voice choked with sobs as she rocked him in her arms.

"Oh, my son—my son! I feared I would never see you again."

Ori waited for the sobs to subside before he spoke. "Why are we on the ship of the Egyptians, Mother? Are we to sail to the copper mines to the south?"

"No, Ori, my little one." Mari released her grip on her son. "When you disappeared, Mahah came to tell us that the Egyptian workmen had taken you to the city of Gubla. In the dark he could not see, and he supposed it to be so. We feared the men would return and bring suffering on the family of Sephar for sheltering us. The Egyptians told of their suffering as slaves, how they were forced to worship gods that were strange to them. When the Ancient One explained our journey, and why we left Babil, the family of Sephar decided to go with us—to accept our God."

She stopped speaking as she looked to the bow of the ship and saw a great half-mooned sail unfurl. The timbers moaned softly as the sail caught the wind; with the men pushing against the pier with long poles, the barge eased into the open water. Propelled by two long steering oars

111

and the persistence of the east wind, the craft left the harbor, pointing westward.

After the stride of the voyage had been set, Ori spoke again. "If Sephar is coming with us, where are we going?"

Mari turned her face to the wind. "We are to seek the land of the Ancient One's vision. Sephar told him of a great island far to the west where Egyptian ships have traded. Perhaps here we can worship God as we please. We will not follow the trade routes to the south and north, for fear of being seen by the Egyptians. We will sail directly west, perhaps losing our way, but Sephar believes he can guide the ship by the star of the north as he has been taught by the Egyptians. Look!" She pointed up into the star-flecked ceiling of the night. "You can see it up there."

Ori wondered how a star could guide the course of a ship across so vast an unknown sea. He remembered when he and Gilgah had stood on the hilltop at Kish and prayed, so close to the stars and God. Now he prayed, asking God to direct their course through the black sea, as the ship moved like a great winged bird in the night.

By morning the wind slackened and the great sail billowed lazily in a dying breeze. After the sunup meal the men took to the oars, and with steady sweeps of the long paddles moved the barge slowly forward. The sea lay peacefully quiet, its blue horizons unbroken by land or pursuing ships. Later the wind freshened, blowing from the northeast. The sail filled again, and the ship moved swiftly without the oars.

By afternoon the sea mounted under a heavy wind. The ship pitched up one side of the swells and down the other. Men and women bent over the rail, white-faced with seasickness. The animals became restless, whinnying and bawling as high waves washed over the sides. The provisions became soaked, except those stored in goatskins and earthen jars.

112

It was agreed that the sea was not dangerous enough to lower the sail and what damage the rolling and pitching of the ship provoked would have to be tolerated. By sailing with the wind they knew the days would be shortened that separated them from the great island to the west.

By nightfall the wind lightened and the whole company relaxed from the strain of the day. Young people clustered at the prow to sing and laugh and talk together. A flute's soft melody drifted out across the water. An old man's voice crooned an ancient psalm. Pagag and Elissa, the slave girl of the Amorites, stood shoulder to shoulder, watching the blazing sun sink farther and farther into the liquid desert.

So the days passed—crowded, restless, drenched with sun and rain. Once the ship was blown off course northward for a day's journey. Then the wind changed; the ship was caught in a western current and taken back toward the intended direction.

On the tenth day of the voyage, Ori climbed again to the top of the two-pronged mast to search for land. Perched there atop the sail's spar he saw, far to the southwest, what looked like a dark cloud hugging the rim of the sky. It faded, then returned, to remain a solid, green mass above the water. Soon the peaked outline of a great island grew before them, crowned with forest-covered mountains.

Maneuvering the craft along the north shore, the men steered toward an inlet, and with the inrolling thrust of the surf ran the ship aground.

It was when Jared and Sephar jumped to the sand to secure the anchor that Ori, standing at the bow, became aware of strange people standing along the shore, silently watching them.

Chapter 12

The Island

ORI'S pulse quickened when he saw one of the islanders come toward Jared and Sephar. The man was short and slight of build, graceful in movement, his long black hair curling about his shoulders. He wore a short, pointed skirt, tightly laced about the waist, and his arms and neck were encircled with bright metal bands. He spoke, but in another language. Sephar answered in Egyptian, but he made no response. He beckoned for Sephar and Jared to follow him.

Ori saw Jared hesitate, then look back to the boat.

"Send the Ancient One here," he shouted to Ori. "He can understand what this man says."

Ori helped the old man out of his hammock and over to the edge of the boat. With Mahah and Pagag's help, Ori gently lifted him over the bow and into the arms of Jared and Sephar. They carried him through the water onto the shore, letting his feet touch the sand before the islander. The two men talked for several minutes, exchanging meaningless words, then finally the islander's face brightened, he smiled slightly as he slowly began to understand what the old man was saying.

Slipping daggers into their belts, Ori and several of the other young men jumped from the barge and moved slowly up the beach to join Sephar and Jared. Since the islanders seemed friendly, the boys' curiosity urged them to find out what was being said. As they came in close, the Ancient One began talking to Jared in words they could understand.

"We are on the island if Idaea, ruled by Minos, a great war lord. We are to go to him or he will be angry." The old man's voice was firm and strong.

Jared looked back at the faces of his family and friends rimming the bow of the barge, then to the circle of strong-armed islanders facing him.

"If these people were going to harm us they would have done it by now." Jared adjusted the leather belt about his waist and touched the sheath of his dagger. "We need food and rest. Perhaps this Minos can allow us these favors." He shouted back to the boat. "If we are not back by sundown you may never see us again. But we will be here before then."

Ori stayed close to his father as the voyagers followed the men of Idaea up a steep incline of mountain trail onto a high plateau. The trail widened into a roadway bordered with olive and cypress trees. Still climbing, they followed the road until it ended in a complex of great stone buildings that hugged the mountainside like a fortress.

The guide motioned for the group to remain on a paved terrace before one of the largest buildings. He ran up a great flight of steps and disappeared through an open door. When he returned, several older men were behind him. Then a powerfully built man with two great hunting dogs came through the door. A tinge of fear pricked Ori as he saw the man come to the rim of the stairway and stare down at him. The dogs whined, sniffing and licking their mouths, ready to leap at a given signal. Ori noticed that the man wore an ankle-length embroidered skirt with a heavily corded waistband. His arms glistened with copper bracelets, and his head towered with a colorful turban topped with peacock feathers. His hard black eyes passed over Ori and his father to the faces of the other men. Extending his palm outward, he spoke in Egyptian, which was repeated in Babilian by the Ancient One.

"Do you come as traders or intruders from the land of Egypt? I am suspicious of men's reasons for coming to my island."

Sephar spoke up, for he understood the king. "We come as friends from the port of Gubla. We seek food and rest for our families and animals. We are not traders, but we bring you the wisdom and learning of the great peoples of the east. My sons and I are skilled in building ships that can sail to far countries. My companions are scribes and merchants who have served the great Nimrod, king of Shinar. They can fashion copper and tin into bronze. By molding bricks from clay they can build towers to heaven. Their women weave beautiful garments and turn fine pottery. Surely we are a people of peace who come seeking your help and friendship."

Minos stared at the men, then turned to his counselors. Again he spoke to Sephar. "If your people possess such great powers, bring them into the shadow of my Great House and we will see if you speak with a double tongue."

Giving instruction to the guide and calling to his dogs, Minos disappeared into the building, the older men shuffling along behind.

By sunset the people of Jared had pitched their tents against the mountainside and lit their evening fires. The animals were fed and tethered for the night; the men stood in clusters awaiting the sundown meal. A group of young women bent over a shallow pool, washing their hair and splashing each other, laughing merrily.

It was then that Minos and some of his court came into camp. He saluted Sephar in Egyptian, then bypassing the men walked among the tents, smelling the food, tapping the bundles of unpacked provisions with a tapered staff. He paused for some time among the animals, noting the auroch calves and the onager colts. Then he passed deliberately by the young women as they dried their hair. He looked from face to face, weighing their comeliness, his gaze finally resting on the flushed features of Milcah. Abruptly he turned away and strode back to the Babilian men.

"It is well that you have come among us," he spoke to Sephar. "You will be a great benefit to the development of

116

my kingdom. On the other side of this island is a beast of a man called Sarpedon who dares to interfere with my trade with the Egyptians and the cities to the north. I must strengthen my position here—build great cities, great fleets. You and your sons can fashion ships with which I can overthrow Sarpedon. Then I can expand my trade with the Egyptians and the Aegean ports. Even to the west, it is rumored that a land lies rich in grains and metals." The lord straightened to a commanding pose. "At sunrise, send your skilled men to the Great House for instructions. I will need a scribe, a planner, a builder, many workmen." He turned back to the spot where the young women had been, but they had now disappeared into their tents. "The golden-haired one; bring her into my quarters by midday."

The men of Jared listened in silence when the Ancient One told them what had been said. Then Jacom, a slow red anger flushing his face, came and stood before Minos.

"We will help you build your ships and your city, but the golden-haired one will not come to your quarters."

Minos raised his head scornfully when he heard the meaning of Jacom's words. "You have no choice. You are but a poor miserable people, dependent on my favor for your existence. If you are not willing to send her to me by midday you will be used as a plaything to amuse my beautiful bulls in tomorrow's festival of the great Earth Mother."

As he spoke a dull sound rose from the ground, followed by a short, sharp shock like the motion of a ship battling a strong wind. The men were thrown backwards, and it was several seconds before they regained their balance. Minos, seeing their fright, laughed sharply and turned to leave.

"As you see, you have angered the Earth Mother. She is allowing the bull of the underworld to toss his horns and bellow against those who disobey the word of Minos. It is well that you trouble her no more."

After he had disappeared into the Great House the people of Jared stood as he had left them, trembling from the effects of the earthquake. The sundown meal was forgotten as they huddled fearfully together, shaken with the predicament they had slipped into.

Jacom's voice burst out. "We must leave tonight. We can act as though we sleep, then slip down the trail to the sea. Our ship is still sound—it will carry us to this land to the west."

"It is a great risk," Jared cautioned. "If we were caught, I doubt he would spare one of our lives."

"We have no choice now." Gilgah pointed toward the towerlike structure at the back of the Great House. "Minos trusts no one."

Down the steps, marching in single file, came a company of men carrying long spears. They marched around the camp, placing themselves equal distance apart and stood facing the Babilians.

"Now we must outwit him," Gilgah said decisively. "We will do our work so well he will not suspect our intentions to escape in ships that Sephar builds. We have done it once; we can do it again."

"But what of Milcah? She cannot play such a game. She is to bear a child." Jacom's voice was a harsh whisper.

"Go into the pen of bulls—just as he says," Jared said decisively. "Wear the heavy leather waistband and leg pads you used with taming the aurochs."

There was a long wait before Jacom answered. "I will do this for Milcah and see if Minos is satisfied. If I survive, he may think of something else."

"We will pray that he will not." Jared spoke reassuringly. "It is time we sought the Lord's direction—before this day passes. Then we can break bread and sleep in peace."

As the cry of the night birds sounded overhead, the voices of the men were heard, one by one, seeking the divine will.

By dawn the men were up, eating and washing, anxious to perform well all of Minos' demands. They even awakened the guards who had fallen asleep, and together they marched up the steps of the Great House and disappeared. Other guards came out of the tower to replace the night watch.

By midday no one from the Minoan court came among the women to take Milcah to the ruler's quarters. And she, fashioning cakes from wheat flour, wondered at Jacom not returning with the men at mealtime. No one dared to tell her why.

It was late afternoon when the festival began. Streams of gaily dressed natives, coming from all the eastern half of the island, flowed into the Great House courtyards. Ori, watching from behind the guards, noticed the elegant ladies with tightly girdled waistlines and flouncing skirts, the long-stoled priests, and sinewy youth descending the palace steps. His eyes wistfully followed the laughing celebrants as the crowd disappeared down an incline to the arena which adjoined the western wall of the palace.

Ori knew something unusual was going to take place because of the tense look on his mother's face and the whispered conversations between Gilgah and Jared at the noon meal when they had slipped several leather objects inside their tunics. He looked at his mother now and saw her face drawn with anxiety and fear, lacing her fingers together again and again as she stared unseeing toward the palace.

Vowing to find out why his mother was afraid, Ori looked at the guards. Their attention was centered on the people hurrying to the arena, a bored look masking their faces.

Casually Ori strolled back through the tents, feigning an interest in feeding the tethered colts. The last guard, close to the mountainside, sat above the animals, high on a rocky ledge. Ori could see that he had been drinking, for a wine pitcher was in his hand and he now sat snoring, his chin low on his shoulder. Dodging below the rocks, Ori crept through the tall grasses, keeping an eye on the second guard who stood several feet away. By moving slowly, selecting the biggest rocks and shrubs for cover, he was able to edge down the moun-

tainside out of sight of the camp and into the trees. Running
for the road, he joined a group of islanders and, losing himself
among them, hurried back up the hill to the arena. Pushing
through the crowd he came to the low stockade that fenced
the arena and crouched between the wooden posts to see what
was going on.

From a high, open balcony overlooking the arena sat the
court of Minos, resplendent in jeweled and feathered regalia.
Ori saw the lord of the island lean across his minister to tip
the chin of a fair-skinned lady, who laughingly drew away
from him. Priests with lighted incense bowls walked back and
forth behind the court, scenting the air. Below, the arena was
filled with dancers, their slender figures twisting and swaying
with the music of drum and lute.

At a clap of the lord's hands the dancers disappeared
into the palace and a group of brown-skinned, lightly built
young men sprang into action. They wore hard leather hel-
mets with strips of cut rawhide wrapped about their hands.
With both hands and feet they began hitting each other in powerful blows to the head, chest, and legs. Some of them went
down, the winner then turning to another until only a few were
left fighting. Gradually these too lay in the sand until only
one remained. He was taken to the foot of the balcony and,
cheered by Minos and the people, was thrown a wreath of red
flowers.

Other youths came into the ring to run races and do acro-
batic stunts that Ori had never seen before. Even girls did
handstands, springing over each other in effortless skill.

Again the lord clapped his hands and the arena cleared.
The hollow blare of a conch shell sounded. The priests and
priestesses came, chanting to the beat of the drums, bearing
fruits and flowers and bowls of incense. Behind them walked
a man with a snake wound around his shoulders. Another
priest bore a small carved figure of a goddess. As the procession passed around the circle of the arena the islanders knelt to

120

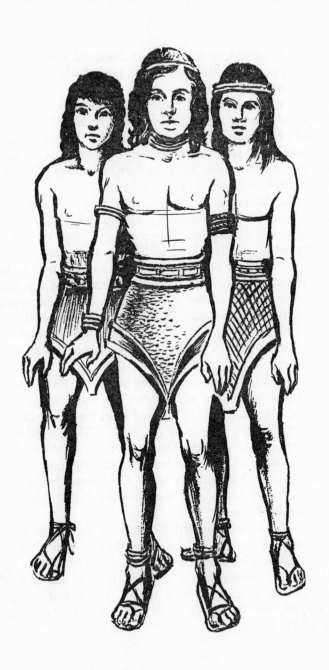

the ground, wailing, and when the priests and priestesses filed up the steps of the balcony and stood behind Minos, the crowd arose shouting.

As the sounds echoed across the mountains, a new door was opened into the arena. There was a breathless quiet when the head of a great brown and white spotted bull emerged, his long horns thrust forward as he charged into the open. Behind him came another bull, then another, all heavy shouldered, thick of neck, with sharp, tapered horns.

Ori hardly breathed when he saw several acrobats jump into the arena close to the bulls. They danced about the long horns, apparently unafraid. Then one of the girls, balancing carefully before a beast's lowered head, put her arms about the horns. With a burst of anger, the bull tossed her over its back. The girl somersaulted over the animal's rump and was caught in the arms of one of her companions. Shouts of approval swept up from the crowd. The stunt was repeated, this time with two of the young men. One of them fell sideways and it was only the swift back pull of a fellow acrobat that saved him from the side swing of the horns.

As Ori watched another young man was thrust into the arena. He wore a heavy, wide leather belt and thick pads upon his thighs. He came slowly forward from the palace door and stood watching the actions of the bulls. The crowd stilled. As he came into closer view, Ori recognized his brother Jacom. Now he knew why the whispered conversations, why the strained look on his mother's face. Cold sweat broke out on his temples and his hands, and he prayed that his brother would not be harmed.

One of the bulls sighted Jacom. He sniffed the ground, bellowing and pawing as the figure before him slowly advanced. With a burst of energy, he began to run, lowering his head for an upward thrust. Jacom leaped sideways, then turned quickly to face the bull again. The crowd murmured disapproval, and Minos sat tight-lipped and frowning at the edge of his bench.

122

Again the bull lowered its head, and the unskilled Babilian caught the horns between his arms and felt himself being thrown into the air and onto the sand, all in an instant. A wild cheer went up from the watchers. Ori's fingers tingled with excitement. Slowly Jacom got to his feet.

Another one of the bulls, abandoned by the acrobats, came snorting close to Jacom. He was a younger animal and with shorter horns and lighter build. After raking the first bull's flanks with the tip of one horn he turned suddenly on Jacom and charged. Jacom had no time to jump aside, but felt a sharp pain in his thigh as he left the ground. Grasping the horns in a deathlike grip, he swung his body up and over, pulling the bull's head sideways and throwing the animal on its back. Jacom was thrown free of the thrashing hooves and as he scrambled to his feet to face the animal again, he saw the wild struggling bull suddenly slump into a relaxed stillness. Its eyes stared blindly into space, and Jacom knew that it was dead.

The other bulls had apparently lost interest in the game, for one was lying down and the other ambled back toward the entrance.

Jacom looked down at his throbbing leg and saw, below the leg pad, a red stream of blood oozing from the horn wound. He looked up at Minos to see if he had accomplished the required entertainment necessary to free him from further exhibitions. The frowning man, moved by the approving shouts of the islanders, tossed him a wreath of flowers. The priests came down the stairs, singing and chanting, bearing a wooden altar. One of them severed the head of the dead bull, placing it upon the altar, while the crowd wailed to the Earth Goddess.

Ori climbed over the top of the stockade and ran to Jacom's side. Tearing the hem of his tunic, he quickly bound the wound in his brother's leg. Bearing much of Jacom's weight across his shoulders, the two walked slowly out the entrance, past the guards, up the flight of steps through the palace, and back to camp. Milcah, waiting there, gave a little cry of fright as they laid Jacom on his bed and dressed the wound with ointment and clean linen. Mari, seeing her oldest son alive, clasped Ori to her, too happy to wonder why these two should be together.

Minos came no more to the Babilian camp. He sent fresh fruit and sea delicacies to Jacom's tent, but he did not withdraw the guards or ease the work burdens of the men. They were his slaves, and he never let them forget it.

By the time the wound had healed enough for Jacom to hobble into the Great House for instructions, a fleet of ships stood, ribs bared, along the northern harbor. Wharves were cut into the ledges abutting the deeper water so that ships could anchor there. Across the coastal plain back of the harbor the outlines of a vast city were visible. Foundation stones, cut with bronze saws, upheld walls where no mortar was necessary. Small factory areas were laid out along narrow streets, providing for the production of bronze and copperware, fine woodworking, pottery making, the refining of oil from olives, the weaving of colorful textiles, the making of wine. Roadways led up the mountainside to terraced gardens of newly planted vineyards and olive groves. All the natives of that end of the island worked from dawn to sunset to make this the trading center of the Great Sea. Minos was ever among them—demanding, commanding, pushing the work ahead.

It was in the month of Ab, when the days were hot and dry over the island, that the subject of escape came to the Babilians as they ate their sundown meal. Gilgah spoke of it first. Ori listened as he lay on his back facing the stars.

"We are no longer free men—but slaves to one man's ambitions. All we have belongs to Minos."

"We are learning new skills—just as we did under Nimrod," Ethem said.

"But we are slaves none the less." Jacom's voice was resentful. "My child will be born in a tent, overshadowed by a tyrant who would kill us both if it pleased him."

"He has been kind to us—in his way," Ethem mused. "I have seen worse."

Gilgah pushed at the thought of escape again. "The ships are almost completed. Soon they will be tested in the north sea. It is rumored that the first long voyage will seek tin and copper ores from the land westward. Is it not true that the barges are being built to hold great cargos and stand high seas?" He turned to the shipbuilder who was now able to understand Babilian.

Sephar nodded. "These barges are ribbed with cypress beams and overlapped with the finest cedar on the island. Their hulls are sealed with heavy resins and their copperplated prows will cut the storms as with a sword. We have added a second small sail to the bow which will balance and guide the ship before the wind. What we have yet to do on the first ship is to install the rigging, and she will be ready to sail."

"Are you suggesting we seize the ships we need," Jacom asked his uncle, "or sail with the seamen of Minos?"

Gilgah shrugged. "It depends on what we agree."

"Do you believe this land to the west was that seen in the Ancient One's vision?" Ori broke in, wanting to be part of the planning.

Gilgah thought awhile before he answered. "I am not sure. The Ancient One has not spoken of the vision for a long time. He has wilted with the summer heat and says little. I fear he will not be with us much longer."

He reached for a cluster of grapes. "If this land is inhabited with idol worshipers I know it is not the place God has made for us. It does lies in the course that was set back in the Valley of the Great Hunter, and we will never know, until we walk its soil, whether it is the promised land or not."

"Then let us go there before the fall months bring storms to the Great Sea," Jacom urged. "Perhaps Minos would trust Sephar and his sons to man some of the ships. The night

125

before the voyage—under the cover of darkness—our people could slip into the boats."

"We still have the Egyptian barge." Ethem chewed on a barley cake. "Why should we wait for the other ships to be completed?"

"I would not trust the weakened vessel to the water again," Sephar said. "Already it is sinking in the harbor, heavy with water."

"What my son suggests has merit," Jared mused. "If it is well planned, we will not have to act as pirates but as unseen passengers—at least until we are safely on our way." He spoke to Sephar. "Would Minos trust you to man his ships on this western voyage?"

Sephar looked to his sons. "I will lay ideas before him that he cannot resist. He will probably send two of his first ships on this trip. My sons and I can so lay the rigging that no one else will know how to use it."

"But there will be his crew along."

"We can handle them. Later we can teach them how to operate the ships so they can return with the cargo, and all Minos will lose are a few stray Babilians." Sephar laughed shortly.

"And the guards? They do not sleep every night," Ori worried.

"But they love wine. We could share a small celebration with them the night we leave—perhaps in the memory of a dead bull." Jared winked at his son and stood to leave. "Sephar will determine the time, and we will lay wine in store—and provisions for a long journey. It will please the Ancient One to see his beautiful land before he dies."

Chapter 13

Moriancumer

O N THE tenth day of the month of Elul, Sephar signaled to Jared. Two ships had passed their tests and were at the wharves, ready to sail.

All that day carriers stacked jars of oil and wine amidships, packing them with wool mats to keep them from breaking in heavy seas. This cargo, when traded for the precious ores of tin and copper, would help Minos become the ruler of the whole island of Idaea. With bronze weapons he could capture the trade of the entire Great Sea.

Crews had been selected by Minos and Sephar and were prepared to leave at dawn.

By nightfall the Babilian camp was packed. The tents that faced the Great House were left standing and the rest tied into bundles. Only choice pairs of sheep and goats, cattle and colts were tagged to make the journey. These would stock new herds once they reached land again.

A great fire was built in the camp area, over which a skewered sheep turned and browned for the evening meal. The women put on their best clothing and tied their hair with flowers. They brought out platters of ripened grapes and figs, bowls of boiled lobster, clam, and tunny fish; loaves of wheat and barley cakes. Pots of honey and mint jam and pitchers of fine wine were spread on mats around the fire. Younger boys brought out their flutes and drums while several of the children began to dance.

Ori, musing by the fire, found it hard to realize they were actually leaving the island. Despite the hardships of his people, he was fascinated by the empire-building dreams of Minos. Perhaps some day he, Orihah, could look out over villages and cities, mountains and ship-dotted seas and know that what he saw was of his own making. He remembered Kib's words, "I'm going to be king—I'm going to be king," and felt this same impulsion to create a kingdom by the strength of his will. In the land westward he might become such a ruler. But the men who served him would not be slaves; they would be free.

A light touch on his shoulder interrupted his thoughts. It was Baba bending above him, her eyes shining in the firelight. So little had he seen of her during the past months he had almost forgotten she existed. He was startled to see how full her face had grown, how tall she was, how soft her hair. . . . His staring look made her lower her head in embarrassment.

"Elissa and Pagag wish to be married. They would like the Ancient One to give them a blessing—but he is so weak." She hesitated. "Perhaps you could ask your father what to do."

Ori looked back into the fire. Why didn't she ask his father? She was perfectly able to. Unwinding his legs he stood looking at her again, actually flattered that she had come to him. "Don't worry about it. I'll find him."

Jared was making last-minute ties on a pack when Ori found him. When he heard the news he went directly to the couch of the Ancient One. The old man raised his head and listened quietly, nodding in approval. He beckoned with a gnarled hand for the young people to come, and when they knelt before him, he raised to a sitting position and spoke the blessing of unitement.

Feasting and dancing and singing followed. Even the Ancient One tapped his fingers to the rhythm of the drums. In their excitement over the wedding, the Babilians forgot their

plan to escape until they saw the guards—smiling and nodding—eager to become a part of the celebration. They welcomed the men into the feast, gorging them on roasted ram and
barley cakes dripping with honey. Then they were given the
wine.

By midnight the singing and dancing ended. The guards
were fast asleep in a drunken stupor while the Babilians—
carrying heavy packs—slipped from the camp and made their
silent way down the mountain trail.

When dawn came, Sephar and his sons were waiting on
the wharf when the crew arrived. Eyes still heavy with sleep,
the islanders unfastened the mooring ropes, scanned the set of
the sail, and pulled in the gangplanks. Just as the ships were
moving away from shore, a lone figure appeared on the wharf.

It was Minos!

"You have no breeze," he called to Sephar. "Is your crew
strong enough to row the ships out into the wind?"

"Oh, yes, my lord," Sephar assured him. "My men are
strong. Once they feel the surge of the oars, we will be riding
with the wind."

"Beat them if they are too sluggish. I want these ships
back in harbor by the harvest moon. The Babilians will have
the city built by then and the smelting furnaces ready for your
ores."

From the helm of Sephar's barge came the baa of a sheep.

Minos shouted, "What insolent pig has answered me so?"

Sephar hurried to explain. "It was only the creaking of
the mast, my lord. We are moving out with a bit of a tide.
Never fear, we will return when the moon is full."

Shouting to his crew to man the oars, Sephar busied himself, singing and laughing as loud as he could to cover any
noises his hidden passengers might make. Slowly the oars
dipped in unison, flashing wet with the dripping sea, forcing
the barges into the open water. A slight breeze caught the
opened sails, easing the strain on the oarsmen. As the light of

129

day swept away the shadows from the mountains, so the two ships of Sephar swept into the wind and gradually disappeared from the sight of the lone man upon the shore.

Little did he suspect how long it would be before he would see the ships again.

For two days, the peaks of the island lay to the south. The sun was hot, the sky cloudless, the wind listless. The small, square sail, no longer needed to hide the Babilian stowaways, billowed from the short masts which leaned forward from the bows—guiding the ships before the wind. Gulls circled over the masts, watching for scraps of food while alongside, diving in and out of the water in great waves, the dolphins followed. Fishermen from the western end of the island came close to wave and shout but were soon left behind.

As the days passed, Ori followed Sephar about, asking why the sails were square; if there should be another sail added above the first—higher on the mast; what would be done if the wind blew against them, thrusting them backwards; how the prow was directed to unknown lands in a given course; how the stars were used as guides. Sephar answered from the wisdom of the Egyptians and his own experience, not always satisfying the boy. When the questions became too involved, Ori would climb the mast and perch on the beam of the sail and search the horizon for his answers. But the sea looked much the same, undisturbed as a bowl of dark wine.

One day a low bank of clouds came out of the northwest. Gusts of wind, pushing against the water, furrowed it with alternating troughs and ridges.

Ori slid from the mast when he felt the motion of the barge change from a gentle pace to that of a charging bull. Within minutes the seas built up into rolling swells. The force of the wind pushed the craft backwards toward the east. Quickly the crewmen lowered the main sail. They strained at the steering oars to keep the ship from turning broadside to the waves. About every tenth wave the prow dipped under

130

green water, then it would climb up, up, up, teeter an instant, and crash down again. Women and children bailed with pots and bowls to keep the water from amidships where the cargo lay. Then men wound skeins of rope through the looped handles of the great jars and tied them to the mast.

Ori, braced against the side close to the women and children, was tightening the rigging when the ship suddenly heeled over as it sank between waves. In that instant he saw something being swept overboard. Instinctively he dropped his rope and grabbed. Pulling and straining with the strength of a man, he worked the sodden object back onto the boat.

It was a girl, gasping for breath, her mouth streaming with water, her hair and clothing drenched. He leaned her against the jars of oil, wiped the water and hair from her face, and yelled for help. It was Baba.

They laid her face down among the packs, working to empty her lungs of sea water, little knowing whether she would live or die. Ori turned to find his abandoned rope but his strength had gone. He stood shaking, his teeth chattering until his knees gave way and he slid down against a jar, his mind crowded with one thought, "Why did it have to be her? Why did it have to be her?"

It was not until the rains came, turning the raging surface of the sea into a silky smoothness, that Ori knew Baba was breathing again. He hoped she would not try to thank him. Right now he did not want her gratitude—or her attention. He avoided her so much that it was days before he allowed himself to speak to her again.

When the storm clouds lifted, a small island appeared to the south. It emerged green and treeless, its ragged hills covered with grasses and rocks. No natives came out to meet them as the Babilians steered onto a wide beach and went ashore to find fresh food and water.

The young men left the ship and set out to explore the island. From a high, rocky hill they looked down into a wide

131

valley spotted with a small lake. Along its western shore were grouped massive buildings made with huge blocks of stone.

Ori and the boys slipped cautiously down the slope, crossed the valley, and crept into the court of what appeared to be a temple. Semi-oval chambers, built in pairs, faced each other with a central corridor connecting them. Looking down this corridor, Ori saw a carved goddess smiling from the top of a great monolith altar which sat in a niche facing them. The goddess seemed to speak, for the faraway hollow tones of a chant came from some hidden recess behind her. Before the altar knelt a small group of worshipers, bowing and swaying to the words of the oracle. When the voice stopped, one of the kneeling figures would toss a small stone into an unseen pit, and following the throw the voice would continue.

So intent were the Babilians in watching the ritual that they did not see the solid line of darkskinned people gathering about them. It was Ori who heard the soft movement of bare feet against the stone paving, and looking quickly behind him, shouted the alarm.

Scattering like deer, the boys ran in all directions, away from the temple, dodging in and out of the great megaliths until they were out of the valley and on their way back to the ships, a few determined natives still following them. By the time they reached the shore, their pursuers had stopped, unwilling to come closer to the strange craft.

Quickly the Babilians boarded their ships and sailed away.

After a four-day sail, land was again sighted—this time to the west. Excitement spread as heat lightning among the voyagers, for this could be the end of their journey—the land to the west—the land rich with copper and tin.

But the land projection did not continue north. It ended as a peninsula, its main body connecting with land masses to the south. When the people of Jared went ashore for fresh water, they found mountains covered with oak and cedar forests, separated with wide, lush valleys and rushing streams.

But there was no ore. Only small pools of dried salt were found which was stored in jars as part of the ship's cargo.

Disappointed, the weary travelers turned back to sea. Burning winds from the south made the air suffocatingly dry. Every day or so, with little warning, gusts of hot air would hit the sails, sweeping the ships about in rising gales, driving them out of sight of land.

It was after a two-day blow, during the month of Tisri, that a full skyline of land appeared to the north. It was not an island but a great land mass stretching from east to west, its snowcapped mountains glistening. Surely this was the land they were seeking.

Eagerly the Babilians pitched their tents along the shore, determined not to leave until the ships were filled with the ores for the furnaces of Minos. Daily they climbed the glacier-fed streams, searching for deposits and outcroppings of discolored sands which might contain nuggets of copper, silver, or gold. Often they returned to camp loaded with sacks of glistening nodules big as bird's eggs, which were sorted and stored in earthen pots ready for smelting.

One day's haul was a sled load of white crystalline rock cut from a vein in the mountain. It was transparent and could be cut in great sheets, one separating from the other.

Bark from a strange oak tree, a tough, light material, was cut in layers and stored in the ships along with the crystal sheets. Minos would be pleased.

The women planted wheat and barley seed, gathered wild figs and berries, hunted the marshes for goose eggs, harvested ripened nuts from chestnut and almond trees, and brought mussels and fish from the sea.

Ori, his brothers, and Pagag, anxious to see the land along the east coast, left the camp one day with spears and packs on their backs. For three days they skirted the oak and cedar forests, high above the sea, finding very little of interest except the beauty around them.

It was the afternoon of the fourth day that they came up over a rise of a mountain slope. Ori saw below them a great curve of coastline cutting back to the north, making a bowl-like gulf at the foot of the mountain. On a plateau, he saw a walled village—built of stone—surrounded with fields of wheat and barley. Flocks of sheep and goats and cattle browsed on the slopes, and men and women busied themselves cutting and grinding the fall harvest.

"And we thought this land belonged to us," Pagag mused. "These are not primitive people—they are like us. See the scythes they are using? And the houses—all made of stone with pointed roofs like many we have seen in the east."

"But these people have walls about them," Mahah pointed out. "Does that mean that they are afraid of enemies? If so, then there are people to the north and west that we haven't seen."

"Or they came on ships as we did," Ori said.

"Should we be afraid of these people?" Mahah asked.

"Of course not!" Pagag moved on down the slope toward the village. "They may be from the island of Idaea."

"But they were not all friendly." Ori held back, remembering past experiences. "There are only four of us."

"As my father often says, 'We can outwit them.'" Pagag never slackened his pace. "We will never know until we find out."

The men and women in the fields looked up in surprise when they saw the four strangers coming toward them. They were dark of skin like the people of Idaea; their cheekbones were high, their frames small. They were dressed in short leather tunics.

Pagag called to them, raising his palm in a motion of peace. They stared back, frightened, then made a sudden rush for the gate. It closed behind them with a heavy thud. Presently it opened again and through it streamed helmeted men, armed with double-edged stone axes and copper-pointed spears.

"So—we are not to be afraid!" Jacom taunted his cousin. "You have not faced a raging bull, have you? But perhaps these people are more civilized and will just throw spears at us. It's your turn to be clever, since you wanted to be so neighborly."

Pagag was not disturbed. "We are not dead yet, my cousin. Who knows, something of great importance may come of this."

He had hardly finished speaking before the four were completely surrounded with men. One of the guards—with spear extended and ax held high—stepped forward, bellowing out a rough command too rapidly spoken to be understood. Jacom moved closer to Pagag, speaking softly.

"This man speaks much as the islanders of Minos. See if you can make him understand."

Pagag thought for a moment, then formed the words he had remembered. "We," he pointed to himself, "come in peace from great Minos," and he pointed to the east. He repeated this over and over until its meaning gradually turned the stern face of the soldier into a wreath of smiles.

"Minos—Minos," he repeated after Pagag. "We know Minos."

Pagag spoke to Jacom from the corner of his mouth. "Do you have any trinkets—gold or copper?"

"I have a bracelet made of silver—and a half jar of wine."

"Pass them to me. These may be our salvation."

When the wine touched the throat of the soldier he closed his eyes and smacked his lips in pleasure, nodding his head for more.

Pagag hesitated. The wine could be used as a bargaining agent, either for trade or, if necessary, for their lives.

"We have a village far to the west—a four-day journey." He held up four fingers in case the guard could count. "If you bring us silver," he held up the bracelet, "like this, we will trade you wine. If you bring us gold," he brought out a nugget from his pouch, "we will trade you oil that will give you light."

The guard stared without understanding. He looked at his companions before he spoke.

"You come—rest and feast with us and give offerings to the Mother Goddess. Then we go for wine." Some of the words were strange to Ori and Jacom, but others they could understand for they were like those spoken in Idaea.

The young Babilians stayed two days in the settlement. They ate delicious foods of the sea and roast wild pig. They even laid a shell offering on the altar of a limestone goddess, careful not to offend their new friends. Then they began loading a flotilla of leather-covered boats with articles of trade. Besides chunks of copper and silver, they stored jars filled with soft, bluish-white crystalline metal into the boats which had been brought from the mountains to the north. This was the treasure sought by Minos, the coveted tin ore, which when melted with copper would produce bronze. And this was not all. Among the discarded earth clods back of the smelting

136

pots, Jacom and Pagag found the silver-white streaks of the metal used to make the Amorite spear. It was iron ore.

Later, facing the rising harvest moon, the two camps sat about the evening meal. Oil flares, stuck in the sands, lit up the feast, delighting the people of Ilici—as the neighbors from the east called themselves—for now they understood the need for oil. As jugs of wine were passed among them, music from soft flutes drifted over the rhythms of the drums, drawing the younger ones to dance and sing for the guests.

By dawn the ships of Minos sailed away, loaded with the treasures of a new land. They still carried enough oil and wine to trade with the settlements to the north. Several of the Idaean crew stayed behind, not wanting to leave the Babilian daughters, but their places were taken by Ilicians who wished to return to the land of their fathers.

By the time spring came, and Milcah's son had been born, the Babilians became dissatisfied with their campsite. The soil on the mountainside was poor, yielding little grain from the fall crops. They also feared the return of the ships of Minos, for by now the fleet could be finished and bristling with bronze weapons.

Several small boats were built, ribbed with cedar and covered with leather. Bundling their belongings together again, the wanderers sailed westward along the shore of the new land, confident they would find a suitable valley in this direction.

They had been at sea only a few days when the winds came upon them, pushing them toward a towering rock projection where the roaring waves beat violently against it. Hastily they lowered their sails and rowed to the south and west—as through a gate—for land barred their passage further to the south. With winds blowing from the east, then from the south, the boats followed the coastline to the north, going in a great curve of the arm of the sea into the mouth of a river.

Up the river lay a lake, and to the side of the lake lay an island, and on the island the wanderers pitched their tents and called it Moriancumer—land given by God.

Chapter 14

The Last Voyage

ORI was sixteen years old. He was tall and brown, hard of muscle, his face narrow and angular, his head crowned with dark, curly hair. He was no longer a shepherd boy following the herds. He and his brothers lived as young lords, sharing spacious quarters in a complex palace whose terraces and gardens covered the whole island. Daily he was among the ships that sailed up and down the coast, gathering riches of the lands to the north. He helped unload the ores brought down from the mines of the upper mountains and watched over their refining. He supervised the plantations that lined the river where crops of wheat, barley, figs, and olives were harvested. Often, he would be seen to stop in his work, his dark eyes looking out toward the sea.

One day when he was coming down the pathway from an upper vineyard, Ori passed the cone-shaped sepulcher of the Ancient One. There beside the tomb, with his graying hair tumbling over his hands, sat Gilgah. When Ori stopped beside him, the great man raised his head, his eyes filled with tears.

Looking up at his nephew, he asked, "Are you content here in Moriancumer?"

Ori looked at his uncle, suspecting a hidden meaning to his words. "Why should I be discontented? We have food and riches to spare."

"That is true." There was a little pause, then Gilgah stood up. "I have all the food I can eat, yet I am filled with a great hunger." He pressed his hands together behind him and looked across the river valley. "During these past few years I have been content to let the days slip by without the divine light that has led me so many times in the past. I walk around and around in a deep pit, doing the same thing over and over, not trying to look up or climb up to the light." He stopped to search the young man's face. "Do these words sound strange to you?"

"I am not bound by walls—only by the sea," Ori answered with a shrug. "It is so lonely here—with just us. I keep thinking of the people we left behind. They had ships and cities. They traveled across mountains and rivers to see each other— to trade, and build, and have excitement. Here, we do much the same thing, over and over. We see the same faces, think the same thoughts. I want to be with other people—to marry a beautiful daughter of some great lord."

Gilgah stared at his nephew, not realizing how the boy's ideas had changed. "You live as a prince. There are riches here—all that you can manage. True, you have no beautiful wife, but time will change that."

"If I could return to the island of Idaea I could bring back a wife with shining black hair, milk-white skin, and a narrow waist. But Father would never allow me to sail eastward."

"Have you considered Baba?" The older man looked slyly at Ori.

Ori flushed, taken unawares. "Her skin is much too dark," he said quickly. "Surely someday ships will come from the east carrying beautiful women. I shall wait for them."

"Just as the Lord waits for us to find the promised land," Gilgah mused.

Ori looked up in surprise. "Is not this the promised land?"

"You know it is not," Gilgah chided. "Has it been so long since the Ancient One died that you have forgotten?"

"Three years ago, in the month of Adar, just after Milcah's second child was born."

"True. We do not forget the time of his death, but we

139

do forget the words that he spoke as he slipped away. He died before he saw the beautiful land envisioned in his dreams. And his message keeps burning in my mind. Over and over it comes, almost as regularly as the sunrise. 'Seek the promised land, my son. Can't you see it there, shining like a jewel in the hand of God? It is waiting, waiting, waiting.' I know this is not the land which he saw, yet all this time I have been too cowardly to acknowledge it. It is a fearsome thing to launch out into the unknown seas, to be covered with great waves, to be driven by treacherous winds, especially when our loved ones might be swept away."

Ori, remembering how he had pulled Baba from the sea, stood silent. He too had no desire to head a ship into the mist-shrouded sea that cradled the sunsets. He would willingly go east or north or south, back along the shores where he had been.

So to please his uncle and to steady his own uncertain motives, he said, "If it is God's will, he will protect us."

"Yes—if it is God's will." Gilgah picked up his cedar staff and turned up the path down which Ori had come. "I am going up into the mountains. Up there I will find out for myself if God is displeased with me." He stopped and looked at his nephew. "Come with me, Ori, as you did in Kish."

"Oh, no," the boy blurted out. "I cannot go with you this time. The latest ore cargos need to be unloaded. There is no time now." Haltingly he waved at the older man, unwilling to involve himself in such a spiritual examination. He watched Gilgah disappear among the rocks and evergreens, feeling that somehow his uncle was foolish to lose himself on the mountainside. The loneliness of the colony must have sapped the man's reasoning. Yet each day Ori came back to the tomb to gaze up through the rocks for a glimpse of a man who wanted to find his God again.

It was on the seventh day that Ori saw Gilgah coming slowly down the path, his shaggy head held high, his face shining. As he came closer, Ori saw that he held several rocks in his hands which gave off a brilliant light.

140

"I have talked with God upon the mountain." His voice shook with excitement. "I have seen such things that words cannot explain. I saw the golden land beyond the western sea. We must go there, Orihah. We will never stop again until we land our boats along its shore. We will become fathers of great nations, and you, Orihah, will be one of them." He held up one of the shining stones. "See these? The finger of God touched them. They will bring light to the darkness of our ships. It will be a long crossing."

Gilgah's words changed Ori's mind. Their God was powerful, one who could lead them through many difficulties—across many waters. Ori was wrong to have doubted this. He would dream no more of sailing to Idaea to look for a fair-skinned wife.

That night Ori walked with Baba in the gardens, forgetting what he had said about her sunburned skin. She was no longer a gangling girl but a lovely young woman, filled with grave thoughts and quick laughter. Despite the quarrels they had had as children, she responded to his inner thoughts with warmth and understanding. The night stilled, and the moon disappeared before the young couple parted and left the garden.

In the days that followed, Gilgah and Sephar bent over designs and materials, determined to create ships that would withstand great winds and waves, that would hold their finest flocks and have space for weeks of provisions.

They widened the beam and lengthened the keel of the Egyptian design, tapering the prows into a beak. They heightened the sides, curving them inward and designed a protective covering of leather, ribbed with reeds, which would make the hull watertight. The bow sail was enlarged and a double mast allowed to uphold the main sail.

A vessel, following the final design, was constructed and tested in the harbor. The men stood along the shore, delighted to see it sail gracefully with the wind. As a final touch, its hull was swabbed with layers of pitch and its interior lined with strips of bark from the cork oak tree, making it light upon the water.

Several ships were constructed, one for each family group. In the final days of preparation, casks of dried fruit, honey, salt, dried fish and meat, olive oil, cheeses, grains, nuts, and great clay jars of fresh water were stored amidships. Tall grasses, cut and compressed between heavy stones, were made into bales of hay for the choice animals that would make the journey. The remaining herds would be left to graze from the wild growth of the river valley.

So it was that in the spring month of Nisan, when the sun's first light awakened the river birds, the barges in full sail left the river and rowed out to sea. Behind lay a deserted island paradise, its palace halls empty and silent, its riverboats bobbing at the wharf, its gardens and orchards left desolate.

Those who sailed on the ships dared not look back, or they would have wept. Instead, they faced the west and sang songs of thanksgiving.

A favorable wind blew off the sea, billowing the flapping sails and carrying the ships away from the coastline. As the days went by, the winds increased in intensity, often driving the voyagers westward toward the Great Sea, then slackening to a gentle breeze. As they passed the great land mass to the south they felt again the hot, searing winds blowing off its surface. The raging gales sent the ships bobbing and careening over the churning waves in wild confusion. With desperate effort the strongest of the men lowered the sails and lashed the tight leather covering over the openings of the hull. Despite the heavy seas, very little water came into the boats. Below, the families, with the light from the stones brought from the mountain by Gilgah, kept the food and water casks from breaking against each other. Hour after hour, as the fury of the wind drove them through the waves, the weary people of Jared sang their ancient hymns, and in singing, their fears were lifted as they waited out the storm.

143

Finally the winds died, and Ori helped his father untie the lashings of their boat covering. He looked out upon a light blue sea. The other barges were sighted, some close by, others balancing on the horizon but still moving southward. Porpoises played far to the west, appearing and disappearing in the waves.

Then to the southwest a projection of land appeared, mountainous and circled with misty clouds. Jared's ship came closer, for the land-hungry watchers were eager for fresh water and relief from the struggle with the sea. Other islands came into view, extending south and west beyond the horizon, apparently not belonging to any large land mass but standing alone.

It was not until Jared and Jacom had crossed the beach of the second island and were filling their waterskins from a mountain stream that they saw above them through the trees a cluster of strange, circular houses. They were built of stone and centered about a crude temple. Small gardens surrounded the houses; beyond these sheep and goats grazed on the mountainside.

When the men turned back toward the ships a shrill whistle, coming from the area of the temple, rent the air; this was followed by a succession of trills and hoots. Similar calls echoed from the surrounding hills. Then from the houses and gardens, the slopes and forests, came barking dogs and tall, well built natives. The men wore goatskin skirts and had their upper bodies painted with colorful designs. Their hair and skin were dark, their lips thick. They timidly neared the men from the sea, staring in blank disbelief, then turned back to each other, giggling. Strange words passed between them, and several called to the two men, wishing to be understood.

"They are like children," Jared spoke to his son. "Our families need rest and fresh supplies. How do you suggest we make these arrangements?"

Jacom rummaged about in his pouch, then pulled out a small bronze knife. "This is something I learned from Pagag.

144

I'll see if it works for me." He held up the knife, letting it catch the light, then walked around the circle of curious on-lookers before him. When he had their full attention, Jacom motioned that he would trade the knife for food. The natives nodded their understanding, then several disappeared.

From up the slope, a sudden piercing cry of a dog was heard, then was silent. Presently, before Jared and Jacom's astonished eyes, two men came offering the dripping body of a slain dog in exchange for the knife.

Jacom, reluctant to accept only this, stood silently waiting.

Jared nudged his son, wondering at this delay. "What else do you want?"

"A bronze knife is worth more than the carcass of a dog, even if we were starving. We'll see what other delicacies they have to offer."

The natives grouped together, then one by one trailed back to their houses, returning later with bunches of long yellow and red fruit, baskets of cheese and boiled fish. These they timidly laid before Jacom and backed off to watch.

Jacom smiled, handed the knife to the tallest man, pointed to the food, and motioned toward the ships that now lay anchored in the small harbor below them.

Quick to understand, the man shouted to the others, and the whole body of natives swooped down the mountainside toward the beach, carrying food and spreading it upon the sand. A fire was built over which the dog was roasted, and around whose flames the entire company of Babilians faced the islanders, feasting together.

Seeking out Baba, Ori sat with her in the shadows, his heart singing again.

After several days—working on the ships, repairing the damaged sails, replenishing the water and food casks—the voyagers set off again. As the ships began to move away from the harbor, two young girls and a young man, decked with shell beads and palm leaves, climbed aboard. Smiling and giggling, they pushed to the stern of the boat and settled themselves there. The natives on the shore waved to them, motioning to Jared with fast, chattering words, then disappeared back up the mountainside.

Puzzled, Jared moved the boat on out to sea, supposing that the three would jump into the water at the end of the island and swim back to shore. But this did not happen. Instead, the young people never looked behind them but seemed content to stay on the boat. As the days passed, they were quick to learn the Babilian language and to explain, in simple terms, the ways of the wind and the sea. Their eagerness and happy ways delighted Jared and Mari, and in the long—often boring—days that the barges crept through languid seas, the natives brought music and laughter to the monotonous hours.

The days spread into weeks, and the winds began blowing from the north. At one time the ships came close enough together for the men to shout to each other. Ori strained for a sight of the dark-haired daughter of Omer. As he called to her, he could hear the giggles of the island girls and his sisters, teasing him.

During a calm, while Ori, Mahah, and the island boy Chinet were swimming around the ship taking a refreshing sea bath, they saw a great, sharp-snouted fish coming up through the waters toward them. Shouting an alarm, they swam back to the barge. Their feet barely left the water when the gaping jaws of the monster opened up below them.

Other great fish appeared, sleek and silver-gray, swarming about the boat, silent and menacing. No one dared to spear them for fear of being pulled overboard. Fresh meat was needed, but fighting these beasts looked too dangerous. Even Chinet shuddered as he watched them.

Ori, studying the fish below him, remembered the day when he had speared the big silver fish in the lagoon below Babil and how that fish had fed the family the night of the flood. Now his family needed food for the sundown meal again.

146

Securing one end of a heavy rope around the prow, Ori made a noose with the other. Signaling to Chinet, and handing him a long pointed spear, he lowered the rope into the water and settled it about the tail of one of the smaller fish sunning itself by the side of the boat. With the loop up on the gray body, Ori gave the rope a sudden, sharp pull and yelled for Chinet to plunge the spear into the fish's side. The great body was stabbed again and again as Chinet stood over it. Ori, with Jared helping, pulled on the rope. Soon the fish's tail was secured to the prow, its head still threshing about in the water. The other fish, attracted by the bloody water, came swimming up, snapping at the wounded prisoner until its head was eaten away. Afraid of losing the rest of the catch, the whole family pulled to bring the bleeding mass on board.

With long, sharp knives, they quickly stripped the flesh from the bones. For their sundown meal they chewed the raw rations of shark meat. They smiled at Ori and Chinet and then at each other, for it was good to have enough to eat again.

When Jared saw that the great fish were still around the boat the next morning, he called across to the other becalmed ships to come. In the next few hours, while the sea churned with the fighting, dying sharks, enough meat was cut and salted to supply each ship for a week.

Suddenly the remaining great beasts disappeared, for the wind had come again.

The sails flip-flopped, then billowed, moving the barges slowly forward. At sunset a storm hit, blowing out of the northeast. It sent the ships scudding over the mounting seas at a pace which made the masts groan and the sails whine and the timbers creak from the violent heaving and twisting. All night it blew, but the men did not lower the sails, for at last they were moving, driven with the winds and currents, closer and closer to their mystic destination.

Around high noon of the next day, bare, rocky islands were sighted to the southeast, but they were too far away to be reached and soon disappeared. Rains came with the wind.

Refreshing water was caught and stored in the near empty water jars. A turtle was brought on board one of the ships, a few fish on the others. When the wind died, the ships glided along through flat blue waters, giving the mariners a chance to mend and repair and rest. The heavy seas and wind had exhausted their strength.

On one of these tranquil days Mahah came to his father, his hand entwined in that of the older island girl, and asked for a marriage blessing. The long black hair, combed and shining, was caught up in a cluster of shells. She wore one of Mari's long dresses and a necklace of gold and silver beads about her neck. She looked much as the other women of the family, except for her full, wide lips and deep-set eyes.

When all had gathered about and prayers of happiness were said, Jared laid his hands on the pair and blessed them. A precious supply of wine was unsealed and they all drank and sang the songs they loved so well. The music drifted out across the water, mingled with the laughter of young voices, until all aboard the ships heard and echoed with their own.

As the shark meat supply dwindled, some of the weaker goats and sheep were slaughtered, one at a time. The hay and grain reserve had almost disappeared. If the voyage lasted many more weeks, all the animals would have to be killed, for they could not live on rope and sea water. Nothing of the slain animals was wasted. Even the hides were salted and cured for lacing on the leather covering of the hull.

Drifting on westward the ships came into a part of the sea that was speckled with patches of yellow-brown seaweed. The hungry people tried to eat it, but even when it was flavored with olive oil, they could not tolerate it. Small crabs and shrimps, taken from its leaves and stems, were more tasteful. All the seaweed that could be reached was raked up and dried and fed to the animals.

After a few days of calm, languid sailing, when the sails hung limp, the air began to change. There were fast-running

148

winds aloft and a dense, sultry feeling in the hot atmosphere. Close to the water, fish jumped wildly about. The first storm warnings came at twilight. Clouds built up and lightning snapped along the horizon. The easterly wind began rising, churning the seas into spumes of waves that began breaking over the prows of the ships. Sensing the presence of an unusual storm, the Babilians lowered the sails and lashed the leather covering securely.

The storm hit with great fury. The barges rose and fell like frenzied beasts, at times being completely submerged by the heavy seas, then bobbing out on an oncoming swell. All night the winds and waves drove the ships westward and did not slacken their mighty thrust until the next evening.

It was during this night that the weak cries of a newborn child mingled with the whine of the storm. Milcah had given birth to her third child.

On the fifth day after the storm, land was sighted to the northwest. It came and went on the horizon, a mystical green veil waving tauntingly before the ships as they sailed toward it. But as the solid earth loomed high in the haze, the wind changed and carried them south and west, out of reach of its emerald shores.

Chapter 15

The Golden Land

A NOTHER day of driving winds pushed the small fleet within sight of several other islands, but steer as they might the voyagers could not break the force carrying them now to the north, then to the west, then to the north again.

A week crept by; all eyes were riveted to the horizons, aching with anxiety. It was after the Babilians were caught in a brisk southerly wind that they drove directly north to a large island topped with mountains and swathed in green forests. As homing birds, the slender prows of the barges cut the rolling surf of the beach and pushed their beaks into the sands.

Everyone cried with excitement. Some of them fell to their knees and kissed the earth. Others knelt and prayed, lifting their eyes to the cloud-flecked peaks, the wide coastal plains hemmed with ruffled foam of the rolling beaches, the groves of palm trees rooted along the water's edge. Fresh water trickled from mountain springs into transparent pools. Ripened fruit, strange and sweet-smelling, hung waiting to be eaten.

In the following carefree days, when little except the drive to fill empty stomachs stimulated the men to move away from the encampment, Ori was left to swim, to lie upon the sands, and to explore the coastal regions with the other young people. Many times he sought out Baba, and they would wander along the beach, talking and singing, marveling over the strange shells and sea creatures washed along the shore.

One day Chinet joined them, and they came upon a rocky outcropping back from the shore. Laughing, Baba ran ahead and sprang on the rocks, calling for a chase. But as she called, several great mottled-green lizards crawled from the crags around her, their high-fringed crests bristling, their scaly heads reared high. Baba screamed in terror.

Chinet sprang forward, picking up rocks and throwing them as he ran. Ori stood paralyzed, not sensing what to do. He could only watch Chinet lift the terrified girl from the rocks—away from the menacing creatures—and run with her back where Ori was standing. Baba stood trembling before him, her face in her hands. Then she shot a frightened look backwards, fearful that she was being followed. But the lizards were still on the rocks.

"Those horrible creatures—they were about to eat me." She shuddered, then turned suddenly and flared at Ori. "And where were you, my great lord? Were your feet rooted to the sand that you could not save me? Here you stand like a thing of stone while I am surrounded with death!"

Ori could not have been more surprised if she had struck him. He looked quickly at her flushed, hostile face, then at Chinet. He had never considered the island boy as a competitor before. But now he saw him in a new light. Chinet was tall and strong as himself, his dark skin clean and glistening, his hair thrust back from deep, serious eyes that gazed anxiously into Baba's face.

Ori looked away, his face flushed with jealousy. "It isn't that I have never saved you from death—if you remember."

"You were afraid. You did not have the courage to face those terrible monsters." Her voice was strained and high-pitched. "If it were not for Chinet I would be nothing but unbleached bones scattered over those rocks." With a

151

swish of her long hair she pushed Ori aside and motioned to the island boy. "After this I will not trust myself with one who is such a coward."

Ori was too hurt to answer. His throat ached, and his ears rang from the fury pounding inside him as he watched the boy and girl disappear around the beach. It was enough to experience a helplessness in the face of danger—particularly when Baba was involved—then to have it flung in his face in favor of a mere island native! He vowed he would kill every one of the repulsive monsters with his bare hands. He would show this Baba that he was not afraid.

But when he charged at the great scaly creatures they scurried away from him behind a ledge and disappeared into a foreboding cave sheltered by overhanging vines. He went no further but turned and threw himself upon the sand of the beach, determined that never again would he seek the company of the daughter of Omer.

It was while he was lying face to the sky that he saw a great golden bird soaring high above him, its movements effortless and majestic. It made him think of helmeted kings and golden temples, the tower of Etemenanki reaching to the heaven, the busy streets of Babil filled with dancing, singing people, the wide sweep of the Euphrates as it circled the shining city. His mind went back to the day of the great storm when he had crawled into the courtyard out of the rain and heard the words of his uncle Gilgah and the Ancient One and the wonderful things that were to happen in his life. Now he remembered these things and tears rolled down his cheeks, for he felt he had been betrayed. Not only had he just been called a coward but in this strange, new land he could never become a leader of men. There were no great cities here, filled with dancing and singing people. How could there be streets and temples and towers and priests and scribes and merchants in a land so desolate and alone? Here were only the members of his family and those of their friends. How could it please God to bring them here away from the great peoples of the east?

By dawn of the next day, the barges were loaded with fresh supplies and rowed out to sea. For this island lay many days to the east from the land designated in Gilgah's vision. The promised land was more than an island. It was a great land mass spreading as the wings of a bird across the waters, and at its heart the people of Babil would anchor their boats and sail no more.

The seas were smooth as emerald silk. The wind, now from the southeast, blew aloft, billowing the sails as white gull wings against the sky. After four days, the voyagers sighted land to the south, and a shout from Gilgah's ship echoed to all the others that this was the country they sought. This was the golden land lying as a jewel in the hand of God.

The winds did not listen to their desires to land, however, but carried them westward, parallel to the continuous green rim that hugged the southern horizon. For many days they saw islands and inlets out of their reach, then these disappeared and silence replaced the laughter and singing on the barges, for the Babilians feared their promised land had slipped forever from them.

On the tenth day out, while they were sailing close together, thunder clouds gathered along the horizon. The winds changed, and a north storm came rushing at them. So sudden and powerful was its fury that the men had no time to lower the sails or stretch the leather cover. The masts bent as strung bows and the sails careened the ships sideways, almost against each other in the rolling waves. Trying desperately to keep the barges from capsizing, the men clung to the masts, slashing at the sails and rigging with their spears to release the heavy winds. One mast, belonging to Sephar's ship, split from the strain and crashed across the bow, its torn sail and timbers disappearing into the churning sea. The craft swept upward, quavering perilously astride a great wave, then dashed downward, its side striking the stern prow of Jared's ship. Chaos followed. Water poured into the broken hull of Sephar's craft, washing over its occupants as they clung to hull and timbers to save themselves. Wild shouts and strong arms of the men overrode the roar of the storm, drawing struggling women and children up over the side of Jared's ship away from death.

The storm lulled, then commenced again. All the next day and into the night it raged before it finally blew out.

Weary, heartsick voyagers faced the dawn. Their food and water supplies were gone, for many of the casks were broken during the storm. When it was light enough, they counted only three barges. Omer's ship was gone, as well as Sephar's wrecked one.

Ori climbed the mast, away from the misery below him. None of the voyagers spoke but kept their lifeless gaze on the sea. Ori wanted to be alone, even if only a few feet away from the others. His was a grief they did not understand and he wanted to hold it to him, to savor it until it became his life. He would never see Baba again, and despite his harsh thoughts there on the island beach, he felt that a part of him had shriveled and died when Omer's ship could not be found.

As misery ground its way into his thinking his eyes listlessly followed the rim of the horizon, and what was unseen at first became more and more of a reality as his thoughts turned from himself and focused on the long thin line of green and brown that stretched from east to west as far as he could see. It grew brighter as the wind and waves carried them southward until it stood before them, a crown of towering forests, fringed with long, shimmering beaches.

"There's a river!" Ori shouted from his perch. "There to the west! And it has a great island in its mouth, rimmed with orange sand."

A wild cheer followed his words. The voyagers hugged

the bows of the boats. Oars flashed as men pitted their spent strength against the remaining space between them and the shore. Some of the young men jumped into the sea and swam with the waves to the island beach where they lay panting, exhausted, in the sunlight.

In the days that followed, Ori worked with the men, clearing and burning away the underbrush of the island and felling the trees to make room for crops and settlement areas. He sank the trunks of small trees into the sandy clay to make supports for circular houses which were capped with cone-shaped roofs of palm thatch. Lean-to shelters were made for the sheep, goats, and cattle that had survived the voyage. They fattened on the lush grasses and bore their young among the rushes.

Seeds were planted by the women and children, including some brought from the Valley of the Great Hunter—the small white seeds. The rains came, the sun shone, and the fruits of the first sowing were shared. The leather-faced men smiled as they ate the hot meal cakes and leaned back in satisfaction. The land was good and bore abundantly.

One night, as Ori walked alone along the beach searching the horizon for a fleck of white that might mean the sail of the lost ship of Omer, he saw a blazing glow on the western horizon. The sky seemed on fire, and the ground of the island shook for an instant, then was still.

Ori ran to the hammock of his father. "There are mountains over there. Could they be pouring out fire from their bellies? I have heard the men of Idaea speak of this."

Jared and all the colony gazed and wondered at the strange fire.

"They call it a volcano," he said.

"I would like to see it better." Ori turned quickly to his father. "Let some of the seamen take me there. One of the boats is still strong. Perhaps we could find gold and silver there—and iron."

"It is too dangerous." Jared set his jaw. He was not willing to go to sea again.

"The sons of Sephar could man the boat," Ori persisted. "They do not mind the sea—they were born on it."

Reluctantly Jared looked at the shipbuilder's sons who nodded their agreement, then swung back to the comfort of his hammock. "Have it your way, my son. You've survived all previous encounters with death. There seems little reason to forewarn you of another."

Ori, sailing along the coast the next morning with the sons of Sephar, came upon another river emptying into the sea. This was edged with great forests where snowy-white cranes flapped from the shallows to perch among the upper foliage. Brilliantly colored birds flitted from tree to tree as they passed, cawing and hooting at the movement along the shore.

Gradually the trees thinned, and long stretches of limestone rocks separated the forests as the land began sloping toward the mountain ridges. White smoke could be seen, curling from the highest peak. The blazing glow of the night before was gone. Layers of cooling lava could be seen where it had boiled, smoking and angry, over the lip of the volcano. Rain-gouged crevices scored the rocks below the lava revealing outcroppings of shining rock, glittering black, green, and white in the distance.

So intent was Ori on the unfolding of the volcanic structure that he failed to notice a ridge of rocks jutting out as a crooked finger in the curve of the coastline. He felt the boat keel scrape bottom and list to the right. When he searched the water to see what caused the trouble, he saw the battered remnants of a wooden ship caught among the rocks. Forgetting the danger, he jumped overboard onto the reef and, pushing with all his strength, shoved the craft into deeper water. Then he looked to the coast and, calling for the others to follow, leaped from rock to rock until he reached the shore.

Calling the name of Baba again and again, he ran along the fringes of the forest and the coastline. He saw no sign of life, heard no answer to his call except the cries of the birds overhead. As he stopped to rest, it suddenly came to his mind that this wrecked hull on the rock could be what was left of Sephar's ship. At the thought he paled and stood bewildered.

Then, resolving not to return to the ship without what he sought, Ori trotted through the trees bordering a rising ledge of rocks and found an opening to a cave.

Beyond the cave opening, in a sheltered clearing in the trees, was Baba, her long black hair wound as a crown about her head, her body clothed in dressed goatskins. She was kneeling beside a grinding stone, crushing grain, and around her sat her mother and younger sisters flattening small cakes of meal with their open palms.

Hearing his footsteps, she turned and seeing him there she grew as white as crane's feathers, her work slipping from her fingers. With a little cry, tears flooding her eyes, she sprang to her feet and moved slowly toward him, believing and yet not believing that what she saw was real.

Reaching out, he ran to her, grasping her fingers in his hands, feeling the longed-for nearness of her tears against his cheeks.

"I dreamed you would never find us." Her voice broke, then steadied itself. "Every day I walked along the rocks, thinking your ship would come—that you would find us here. But as the weeks went by and my father and brothers went up the mountainside and planted their crops and learned to love the land, I knew we would forever be lost to the rest of you. Then, last night, when the great mountain shook and fire came from its mouth, I knew I would rather die than be left in this lonely place."

She leaned her head against his shoulder and cried softly.
Then she brightened. "You must see the mountain. My
father is up there now, seeing if the fire came down upon
his crops. They lay in a tableland above the trees along the
mountainside." She waved to her mother. "There is time."
And before Ori could move to follow, she had darted away
through the trees and called to him from a trail above the
ledge.

Later, hand in hand, they climbed through flowering
shrubs and great tall trees, fragrant and sweet smelling. As
they went higher, the air became lighter and breathing became
easier. Misty clouds swept before them, leaving them
shrouded first in fog, then abrupt sunlight. As they looked

below them they saw in the curve of the seacoast the tiny prowed ship bobbing at anchor, and to the right the plateau covered with fields of grain. High beyond them, smoking passively, rose the gorged summit of the volcano, vapors of steam billowing from its gaping wound. Lava streamed down a trough in its eastern slope, stopping before it reached the fields of Omer.

"Up there," Baba pointed to the outcroppings of shining rocks in the cliff walls, "is where my father found the beautiful stones. Some are shining black and pink, hard as flint. Others are pale green and blue and white; while others are crystal clear like seawater. There is gold there, and iron ore. My father loves it here and never wants to leave." She looked up at him quickly. "But I will leave if you will take me."

Ori's love swelled within him until he felt he could hold no more. Clasping the girl to him he looked out across the great valleys, the fertile fields, the rivers woven as silver threads through dark forests.

"I will take you with me, and you will be my queen." His voice strengthened as he dreamed. "Out of the shining rocks I will build you a beautiful throne. I will crown your head with silver filigree, set with precious stones. Your neck will be hung with golden pendants and crystal beads. Some day my father and Gilgah will be feeble with age and unable to guide the people of Babil any more. With you beside me I shall lead our people to do great things. We shall dry the island clay into fine bricks and with them build a great tower, just as in Babil, and day after day, the tower will grow until it reaches heaven. But there will be no temple for Enlil or Baal or the Earth Goddess. Our temple will be built to the God who brought us to this land. We shall bring him the finest fruits of the fields as an offering of thanksgiving. We shall send boats up the rivers to explore new settlement areas. Cities will be built. Fields of grain will wave in the sun and spread across the land as a great wave of the sea. I shall

159

write the record of our people, just as my father has, and if God will bring other people to this land they will read of our flight from Babil. Our sons will grow and take their place as leaders of the people."

Ori paused as he thought of what he had said, then turned and smiled at the girl. "We shall name our firstborn son Kib—Kib, my childhood friend, who wanted to be a king." He looked out across the sea. "Perhaps by now he is a king, somewhere along the valleys of the Euphrates. But I do not envy him. I would rather be here."

With this revelation of understanding, Ori realized that his ambitious dreaming had constructed the fulfillment of the prophecy of the Ancient One. How simple it seemed now that he had visualized it in his mind. The work that he and his brothers would do, the cities they would build, would be but stepping-stones to the generations that lay ahead when all the land would be covered with their descendants—a new nation.

So Ori dreamed, and when he returned to the island at the mouth of the river—his ship laden with the riches of the mountain, his arm encircling the shoulders of the lovely Baba—he came before his father and, kneeling before the aging patriarch, asked of him a blessing.

Jared, his voice trembling, his rugged face lifted to heaven, placed his hands on the heads of these he loved and prayed.

The sun broke through a rift in the drifting clouds, spreading a shaft of yellow sunshine over the kneeling figures. And high in the clouds, their wings catching the sunlight, two great golden birds circled lower and lower, their eyes intent on a nest below.